
★

OAK STREET WAS A PLEASANT PLACE TO LIVE....

After Linda got to the top landing and rang the bell, she stooped to pick up the truck, and that was when she heard it. The sound of a shot and, simultaneously, over the place where her head had been, a swoosh of air, a blast. Her fingers closed hard around the truck. It was a cheap tin one; a ragged fender cut into the tender skin under her thumb; she felt the spot of blood before she saw it. For an instant, that blood trickling down her hand seemed the worst aspect of her predicament. Then she saw herself as she must look to an observer. A woman crouched over a straw mat who can't decide whether it's better to stay down or, with a semblance of dignity, to regain a standing position.

★

"Borgenicht develops character as well as suspense without missing a turn of the screw in building tension."
—Washington Post Book World

"It's doubtful that there's anyone around more accomplished at the craft."
—San Diego Union

NO DURESS

MIRIAM BORGENICHT

WORLDWIDE®

TORONTO • NEW YORK • LONDON
AMSTERDAM • PARIS • SYDNEY • HAMBURG
STOCKHOLM • ATHENS • TOKYO • MILAN
MADRID • WARSAW • BUDAPEST • AUCKLAND

NO DURESS

A Worldwide Mystery/October 1992

First published by St. Martin's Press Incorporated.

ISBN 0-373-26105-5

NO DURESS

ONE

OF COURSE Linda Stewart understood about the possibility of disaster. She was aware that as you relish your good fortune, you should also take care to distrust it. Life had taught her that while one part of the mind enjoys the current luck, the other part might as well prepare to hear the worst. In short, she knew that alertness had best be the counterpart to contentment.

That is to say, she knew all this, and she didn't know it. Since the good fortune she was enjoying was no more than her due, why should she distrust it? She had worked for it; she deserved it. Indeed, she'd have held it churlish to taint her great pleasure by being skeptical of it. If she was alert, it was to the benign options open before her, and only to them.

So when the girl came into her office to give the ultimatum, all she felt at first was a mild disorientation. The girl was saying something ugly, that was surely clear as Linda sat at her desk surrounded by books and pamphlets and insistent piles of paper, but it was an abstract ugliness. An ugliness that was incompatible with any future she had confidently projected. Her own voice, answering the girl's urgent one, held only a cautious perplexity. "Marylou, I don't understand."

Marylou had short bristly hair and a flat round face from which, as she spoke, a lower lip protruded. "The law says I can do this. Revoke my consent any time before the judge has signed the adoption orders."

"No. The law says you have the right to a custody trial. One that under the circumstances you might very well lose."

With an air of purposefulness, Marylou molded herself into a truculent stance: hands on hips, legs set apart, head thrust forward. "I'm entitled to have my own baby."

Baby: that did it. Marylou hasn't barged in at ten o'clock on a chilly October morning to discuss rights and entitlements and adoption orders. She's talking about a real child. Someone with flecks of green in her deep brown eyes, and the suggestion of a dimple in her left cheek, and a shining cap of dark hair starting to replace the birth hair that fell out. And also—a cherished development—an ability to indicate a distinct preference about how she should be held and who is doing the holding.

Linda stood and came around the desk. Erase any taint of officialdom. "Marylou, I think I know how you feel. You're longing to see her, isn't that right? You feel a deep urge to pick her up, cuddle her. It's natural. Or anyhow it's natural for someone as loving and sensitive as you. That's why from the very beginning I talked about visitation rights.''

"I don't mean visiting." The girl slipped out from the touch of Linda's arm. "She's mine. I want her for good."

For an instant, a paralyzing pain behind her eyes. Then she straightened. What goes on here! She's Linda Stewart, senior counselor of the Riverview Center for Teen-Age Counseling and Reproductive Health. She can handle things. For years she's been handling girls like this. Guiding them so they don't realize they're being guided, coaxing decisions from those unfit to do any deciding, offering solutions in the guise of furnishing options. She has not just done this for a dozen years, she has taught others the tactics. She's a pro. Someone who has given the guidance of teenage sexuality a good name.

"Marylou, let's sit over there."

"I have to get to school. I borrowed someone's car to come here. I have algebra at one." But she let herself be steered to the two chairs on the side of the room.

All right, they're sitting side by side. Steady, steady. "Now tell me about it."

When the girl leaned back, her breasts jutted out under her red jersey—the breasts that five months ago had been bound to prevent the unneeded milk from leaking out. "I've changed a lot, since the baby was born. I did a lot of thinking. So now I thought it over and it's definite. I want her back.''

"Well, let's talk about that a little." Her guidance counselor tone. Cheery. Neutral. "You've probably been seeing babies of that age. Lying there in the carriage, they look darling. You imagine, why wouldn't you, what fun it would be to have her in your own house, buy toys for her, maybe dress her up in something cute. Marylou, isn't that right?" Don't let that expressionless face deter you. Keep talking. "But believe me, it's more than that. I'm not even thinking of the years ahead. I'm taking about right now. She has a touch of colic. Not bad, but after she drinks a bottle, she gets these cramps. Sometimes you have to spend half the night walking her up and down. And in the daytime too. All I mean is, it's constant. A steady need for attention, day in and day out. So who'd take care of her when you were finishing high school? Who'd get up for the two A.M. feeding? Who'd be there every minute?''

"You don't stay with her every minute. You're here at the Center all day.''

Touché. "But Marylou, my God, I can afford a high-priced nurse. The woman who comes in from eight to six—do you know what her salary is?''

Marylou slipped her hands into the pocket of her jeans.

"I moved to a bigger apartment so the baby has her own room,'' Linda went on. "I bought a washing machine and dryer. Now it's getting to be winter, there's a carriage with a hood for when she goes outside. You know, just laying out money for all the equipment . . ."

"You mean, because you're richer, you should have her?"

Richer: that justifiably derisive word, invited by the carelessness of her own remarks.

"Anyhow, I don't have to worry about equipment. My girl friend's sister has all that stuff—her kid is almost two. She said she'd give me everything." When Marylou paused, a look of animation spread across the flat features. "By next summer, the kids can play together. We'll be like, you know, an extended family."

Something like a shiver went down Linda's back. She got up and stood next to the window. "Marylou, you say you have algebra at one. Tomorrow you'll also have algebra at one. Are you planning to drop out of school?"

"I'm doing better this year. A *B* average, just about. All I need to graduate is to pass English and math. Anyhow"—the disdainful hands back on her hips—"I've been looking into places for day care. There's a good one just ten blocks from my house. Other girls manage like that."

Well, yes. It's how countless babies grow up. The makeshift arrangements. The shifting caretakers. The slapdash protection.

"Last week the baby had a low fever. It lasted five days. Day care doesn't take them if they have a fever. How would you feel about staying home with a sick baby for five days?" She stopped. Such nonsense. Day care. Washing machines. A carriage with a hood...that catalogue of the inconsequential. Besides, it came to her what kind of terms had fashioned their discourse. A baby. A kid. A child who is nameless. A child whose natural mother, if she regained possession, would have the right to rename it. Elena Stewart would no longer exist. In Marylou's mind, she didn't now exist.

"Marylou, what about you? Do you really want to mess up your whole life? I remember what you said when we first met. You're good at sewing and making clothes, you want to go to—designer school, isn't that it? Four years there, and then a job, and then maybe, when you're twenty-four, twenty-five, get married. Your own script—you were the one who wrote it. But now—oh, my dear, for a young girl like you to tie yourself down."

A young girl, but possessing an independent spirit. It was, indeed, what had caught her attention. Marylou had been Fran's client, and Fran had come in one day to talk about her. "This interesting girl. I went through all the usual with her, three sessions, good solid discussions, and none of it changed her. She knows exactly what she wants. To have the baby. Oh, I know—it's what plenty of them at first think they want. That fifteen-year-old girl I saw yesterday. 'I want me one,' she said. 'I'll be touching my friend's stomach, and I think, Oh, I want me one so bad.' Marylou isn't that kind of dimwit. If I've sized her up right, she can make her own decision. It'll be an awesome experience, is what she says. Awesome, her word, natch. No, there's no question of marriage, the boy I understand isn't even in the picture. He's in college and he dropped her, she doesn't even intend to tell him she's pregnant. And no support from parents, the mother is dead and the father seems to be remote. Also, she has no illusions about what she's letting herself in for. What it will be like to march around Plains High School in her ninth month of pregnancy. But she's still determined. There's something cocky about her. Not exactly ingratiating, but cocky. Seventeen years old and she intends to have the baby and then she'll give it up—her expression again—to someone worthy."

Someone worthy. It was a phrase to stick in the mind. It stuck in Linda's mind for a couple of months, while she followed, with strenuous casualness, the progress of Fran's client, and one day at lunch she let slip the words that she knew had been destined from the beginning. She wanted to be that worthy someone. She, Linda Stewart, who lived alone, who had never changed a diaper or stirred a formula, found within herself at the age of forty-two the deep wish to adopt a child. Yes, Fran, I know exactly what I'm doing. So Jay Earling, being the lawyer for the Center, was consulted, and some assiduous research was undertaken concerning the health and intelligence and mental stability of both the girl and her defecting boy friend, and at last a meeting was arranged at which it was agreed that Linda Stewart would pay all the medical expenses in connection with the birth of Marylou's child, in return for which the child would be given her for adoption.

"The way you described it, you have such a wonderful life ahead of you. Full and wonderful. Some day, Marylou, you'll have other children."

"Now I want this one."

That streak of stubbornness—all the research in the world can't tell you when it will flare up. "Marylou, who else have you talked to about this?"

"I told Mr. Earling."

Ah. "And what did he say?"

"He said if I'd thought it over carefully, it would be up to me."

Damn you, Mr. Earling. "What about your father?"

"It's not any business of his. He never lifted a finger for me all the time I was pregnant. He didn't care if I had the baby or not."

Marylou spoke with her first touch of emotion, and Linda remembered that father. They had met, a chilly encounter, during the early negotiations, and again, very briefly, in the hospital: a man who in the face of a daughter's crisis cultivated rigidity, indifference, sanctimonious aloofness, as if these constituted the components of paternal rectitude. "Well, what about—what was the boy's name? Gary? Gil?"

"He's not in this. He's off in college someplace—one of those. He doesn't even know I had the baby in the first place."

"Marylou, if it's you alone, you decision, no one influencing you, can you tell me what made you change your mind?"

That surly conviction, spreading over the round young face. "I just did."

"After five months, there must be some reason."

"There's something special goes on. Bonding. All the time I carried the baby, it was happening. I've been thinking a lot about that. Besides"—her defiant stance again—"I'm the birth mother, I don't have to give a reason."

True enough. It was what Linda had explained to countless others. "They're not obligated to give a reason. It can break your heart, but the fact is they don't have to furnish any kind of rationale or justification. Just remember that. Any time till the judge signs the final papers, they can assert their rights. You've painted the room and bought the toys and pored over the books on child care, your heart twists with joy when he squeals at the sight of you entering a room, and then bang, the dream is over. Good-bye baby. Good-bye happiness. And there's not a damn thing you can do. It doesn't happen often, but it happens.''

Well, why, having laid down the line to others, did she not embrace it for herself? Ah, but with her and the seventeen-year-old who was the birth mother, it was going to be different. Using all her persuasiveness, her exquisitely honed understanding, she had delineated the difference from the start. They would keep in touch, she and Marylou. Linda would be the child's mother, the legal mother, the mother for all intents and purposes, but Marylou would not be a complete stranger to her child's upbringing. On birthdays, there would be cards. From time to time, pictures. Even if, as seemed likely, they no longer lived in towns twenty miles apart, there would be, if Marylou wanted them, arrangements for yearly meetings. "You see, Marylou, you're not writing her out of your life forever. You'll know how she's growing up, what she's doing, what she looks like. As for her, when she's seventeen, eighteen—that is, as old as you are now— she won't fall into that panicked resentment that's inevitable when the adopted child can't find out about her past. She'll know who bore her; the information will be available to her. She'll understand that her natural mother loved her very much but was too young herself to give the ongoing care that is every child's right. Any time she wants, she'll know she's free to see you.''

So reasonable. So civilized. Such a model of generous deportment. And so responsive to the canons modern expertise has cunningly developed. Only here is Marylou with her hands thrust into the pocket of her jeans and her face fixed in surly resolve as she says she doesn't have to give a reason.

Linda drummed her fingers on the window. *Do you really want to mess up your whole life?* That exploration of feeling, at once dignifying the predicament and helping to clarify it, that is part of the guidance counselor's standard arsenal. How do you feel about asking your boyfriend to use a condom? How do you feel about having your mother find your birth control pills? How do you feel about being pregnant? All delivered in the cool, nonjudgmental voice calculated to assure the client of the counselor's impartial interest and also to give her the self-esteem necessary for making a sensible decision. But this counselor does not feel cool or nonjudgmental at all, nor can she remotely pretend to impartiality. She is consumed with a scorching judgment, which is that the decision Marylou has made is horrendous, and behind her eyes the pain is so great she can contain it only by turning her back completely on the girl.

"I'll fight this, Marylou, you have to know that. I'll employ lawyers, psychologists, child care experts. Talk about bonding. I'll explain the bonding that's gone on between me and the baby so far."

The girl spoke in her flat voice. "So go ahead. I'll tell them what you said when that other girl wanted her baby. The one you testified for. You said the papers were signed under duress. You said it was a kind of coercion. You said a birth mother has a moral right to change her mind. You said"—a glance at a piece of paper she took out of her pocket, but that didn't change the impressive flow—"You said acquisition of a child by pregnancy and birth is more compelling than acquisition by any other means. You said, this I remember, I thought it was pretty neat, you said contractions are just as important as contracts."

Linda felt herself gasping, as if the room held insufficient air. However, Marylou had got hold of all that, she herself had undeniably said it. What a memorable witness she had been, escorted ceremoniously into the courtroom, speaking up for the teenage girl against the couple who sat with their accusing eyes and formidable displeasure in the front row. Now the wave of that impassioned testimony washed over her. She reached out blindly: among all the indubitable defenses, a lifeline to save her.

"Duress. Come on, Marylou. There was nothing like it in our case."

"Oh, I know. You were very nice to me. Came to the birthing classes with me and all that. But I've been thinking that over too. I got too dependent. I felt I owed you something. You were like a mother. It was like I had to be submissive, do whatever you said."

Where in the world did the girl get these ideas? Who had indoctrinated her?

"I'll tell that to a judge. It seemed I had to do what you wanted. But I'm not weak anymore. I don't have to be dependent on someone. I'll be eighteen in March—I can have a baby dependent on me."

There was no gradual shift; inside Linda something suddenly snapped. Why did that happen? Defeat was by no means inevitable; there were still plenty of arguments to grasp at, those lifelines that were sturdy and accessible. She could point out that the case of that other girl was wholly different, in that the adoptive family had been found drastically wanting. She could refer to the conscientious counseling Marylou had received from Fran and others before she made her decision. She could cite the advantages her own stable position in the community could provide for a growing child.

She wanted none of it. A trial, a publicized trial, Linda Stewart against one of the teenage girls the Center was set up to help...never. She was through with it. She couldn't take it. She could not even bear, all at once, to be in the same room as Marylou. This girl who first had the power to have a child and then, lightly, almost abstractedly, to reclaim it.

She went back to her desk chair, that position of specious authority. "When would you be ready to get the child, Marylou?"

The girl jumped; her nipples jiggled under the red jersey—perhaps she hadn't expected so speedy a triumph. "Mr. Earling said he could pick her up this afternoon."

Mr. Earling is right: if it has to be done, get it over fast. A mechanical transfer, into a lawyer's disinterested arms. Not from her to the girl, surely. In fact, she never wants to see the girl again: the flat cheeks, the bristly hair, the arrogant thrust of young breasts.

"Tell Mr. Earling he can pick up the baby at one o'clock."

Then she heard her own words. The baby: think of that. Already that infant who last week performed the admirable feat of pulling herself up on the side of her crib has receded into anonymity. She has become a footnote, a statistic, a dot in the margin of a graph about unmarried mothers—if Linda can keep thinking of her like that she will make it through.

She picked up the phone. "Debbie? If my twelve o'clock appointment comes in, tell her I'm sick or dead or something. No, I can't explain now, but just do it. Please? You're an angel."

She could, however, explain to Fran. She was longing to explain to Fran. A girl was leaving Fran's office, she heard Fran's voice through the half-open door as she passed: "So let's talk about it next Thursday, Patty, shall we?"—the familiar assurance to someone who has today agreed that yes, she will definitely take her birth control pills or talk to her mother or explain to her boyfriend why she doesn't want to have intercourse, but who will start weakening, finding these resolutions more and more difficult of attainment as soon as she gets out of Fran's stalwart presence, and who therefore by the time Thursday rolls around will need still another boost to her rocky self-esteem, another session with Miss Low.

Linda needed it now. To be able to blurt out her fury. To shriek that they're all rotten, all the confused and treacherous little bitches, so why do we give our lives for them, talk out our heart to them, put our jobs on the line for them, when at bottom they're rotten, rotten. Well, she can't shriek it, and neither can she—as would be inevitable if Fran uttered so much as a word of comfort—break down and weep. Certainly not. Not here in the Center. Not Miss Linda Stewart.

She waved to Debbie, and nodded to the two girls sitting in the front room, and went around to the parking lot, where an expensive sports car was pulling in as she pulled out. The girl was expensive-looking too: a certain air about her hair and jacket and skirt. When the Center was opened twenty years before, it was assumed it would cater to the troubled teenagers of Plummers Bay and Riverview, which were small towns about thirty miles from New York City. It did still cater to the troubled teenagers of Plummers Bay and Riverview. But as the years brought changes, it also found itself making appointments for teenagers from Plains, which was where Marylou lived and where the per-capita income was rather less than the County average, as well as from Mayhew, where the per capita income was high enough to make the book of records and where zoning decreed a minimum of three-acre plots for every house. And thanks to small grants from county and state and more substantial ones from Mayhew families like the Van Cleavers and Stanhopes and Shaws, the original two-room Center was now a solid three-story building that accepted referrals from a dozen schools within a twenty-mile radius and that offered the services, depending on the day of the week, of two nurses, a gynecologist, a psychiatrist, and half a dozen guidance counselors.

And also, from time to time, a lawyer. Someone you automatically called if the words "damages" or "sue" or "malpractice" were hurled in a provocative tone across an unoffending desk. And also, of course, the one who presided if by an unusual combination of circumstances one of the counselors took it into her head to adopt the expected child of a colleague's client.

Jay Earling had done everything right on Linda's behalf. The papers ready on time, the legalities helpfully explained, the necessary meetings arranged with sensitivity and tact. So is it fair to blame him now for the pain that has descended from her eyes to her whole cramped gut? Can he be held responsible for her shaking knees when she gets out of the car, or the tightening in her throat when she remembers that before dealing with him she has to confront the nurse, who is named Claudette?

Claudette was in the living room, rocking the baby. "Linda, you're early. Anything wrong?"

"Put her down."

"She heard your voice. Look, she's smiling already."

"Put her down, I said." She turned away; impermissible, at this point, to see the waving hand, the toes sticking out of the blanket, the curve of eyelash against the pink cheek. Even worse, once the baby sees her, to get the full impact of that convulsed welcome that sends a shudder through the small body and culminates in a joyous chortle in the untutored throat.

Claudette moved toward the baby's room and stopped. When Linda first broached the subject of adoption, her friends told her what the hardest part would be. "Getting help. Forget it. You'll never find anyone who satisfies you. Your heart will sink each time you leave the house to go to work. Or if by some miracle you do find the perfect woman, just as you've got her set in the routines and raised her salary because the baby is mad for her, just then she'll get a call from her family in Barbados or England or Dutch Guiana that her father has had a stroke and she has to go back." They couldn't have been more wrong. From the moment Claudette walked in, all gray hair and starched dresses and broad bosom, there was an alliance; they both stared down at the five-day-old child with the same tremulous pang, the same protective fervor, the same expectant bliss. And now Claudette would know the same emptiness she did. Death... what else could you say? For this child to go back to its biologic mother would be to both of them a kind of death.

She gave the facts with vehement sternness. "No, Claudette, don't say anything. That'll just make it worse. Look, I'm not crying, I can't be crying when he comes, no way he's going to see me in tears. And you'll have to do it. Claudette, please. Don't argue. I don't want to touch her again. You hand her over, I beg you. Just do that for me, Claudette, will you please?"

Claudette's mouth worked, but for a long time no words came out. "Do you want me to start packing?"

Linda sat down. Packing: a new concept. A transfer of not just the child but everything she had bought for it. The flowered undershirts, the terry cloth bibs, the three-colored jacket that was too big but at its marked-down price could not be resisted, the pajamas that were already cramped at the feet, the delicately patterned shirts. And of course the equipment. The crib, the changing table, the bumpers with the clown and his entourage, the blankets, the toys. She had stood with particular deliberation over the toys. Doesn't this frustrate them? Are you sure the paint is edible? At six months, can they really make this go around?

A jolt of anger shook her again. No, not anger. Viciousness. She indulged herself in feeling unabashedly vicious. "Pack the stuff? God, no. Tomorrow I'll call someone. The homeless, the Salvation Army, I don't know, that church two blocks down, they can pick it all up. I'm damned if I'm going to hand it over to her. Let her buy her own stuff if she's so ready, so anxious to have the child. Oh, Claudette, don't look at me like that. I know I'm being shitty, but you know what? I don't want to do a damn thing to make it easy for her. I want her to find it difficult and lousy. And when the lawyer comes I'll tell him just that. From me she gets nothing. Nothing. Just the clothes the baby is wearing."

As it turned out, she didn't tell the lawyer because he didn't ask. The subject never came up. And she had herself under control by the time he walked in. She could even nod with bland politeness at his expressions of sympathy and ask him to sit down because there were some things she wanted to ask him. Such as when Marylou had first talked to him.

"She called me a couple of days ago."

"What did you say?"

"I said it was a very serious thing, something to influence the whole rest of her life. I said she should give it careful thought. I said this wasn't the kind of decision you made in a hurry."

"Why didn't you tell me right away?"

"Linda, I thought of it. The truth is, it sounded so bizarre. One of those wild impulses adolescents come up with and then discard by morning. I never thought she'd go through with it."

She studied him, the agent of her misfortune. A short man who walked with a springy gait and cultivated a bullying cordiality to make up for his lack of height. But with his bright blue eyes and hair curling back from a high forehead, he was undeniably good-looking. The kind of good looks that just possibly would seem hard-edged, calculating, in ten years when he was fifty, but now had a boyish, bouncy charm.

"Didn't you try to talk her out of it?"

"Good God, Linda, of course I did. I said think of the baby. I said look at the advantages Miss Stewart can give, the kind of life, the schooling, the people, the home. There was something inflexible about her. I don't think she was even listening. I felt I wasn't making a dent."

"Then what?"

"She called my office this morning and said her mind was made up."

"You didn't argue with her again?"

He put out his hands in a despairing gesture. "Linda, believe me, I hate this. It's breaking my heart."

Was it? Was it really? Could any outsider appropriate her misery? She looked at him: the ingratiating stare of his eyes, the sympathetic droop of his mouth, and for a second she wanted to shriek. Then she got herself in check. After all, what could he, what could anyone, have done to change things? She'd had a chance herself—she an expert at handling teen-agers—and look how she had muffed it.

"Did she give you any insight into why the sudden change?"

"Linda, listen. They get these illusions about their own capabilities. That's adolescence. Either down in the dumps, consumed with a sense of their own worthlessness, or all puffed up, sure they can get a job or support themselves or pass the test without study-ing.... Why am I talking? You wrote the book. So this girl, I guess she figured it would be a breeze. Other girls bring up children; with one hand behind her back she could do the same."

A sound from inside. The baby chortling? No, Claudette wouldn't let them hear. "I didn't coerce her. Nothing like it. When we made the arrangements, Marylou had a life mapped out, and it didn't include taking care of a child. So what gave her the push, that's what I want to know. What made her decide all of a sudden to change course?"

When Jay Earling stood and walked over to the mantle, he had to strain to get his elbow on it. Ted, her husband of long ago, had been tall, and so were the men she went with after the divorce. Linda was tall herself, a tall, small-boned, slender woman who liked to face a man at her own height. However, you couldn't hold it against a man that the top of his head didn't quite reach your eyebrows.

"She told me that she herself has changed. That having had a baby made her more responsible and mature. Even her marks in school—oh, she told you that too. There was something persuasive about it. Maybe she really means it and just the business of giving birth effected some kind of alteration. Made her suddenly more of person. Or maybe she's deluding us all. Herself included. Anyhow"—he gave up the tussle with the mantel—"you can fight her, Linda, you know that. Say the word and I'll go to bat for you."

"I can't do that. Someone in my position, I can't get into a custody battle with a girl who's a birth mother. She has me over a barrel and she knows it."

When she stopped talking, they both heard the sound. Despite Claudette's efforts, definitely a squeal of pleasure from that other room. "Linda, I forget. How long is it since you got the child?"

A lifetime. "Five months."

"So little. There could be...I mean, right now you're hurt, you're angry, you don't want to think about it. Believe me, I can understand that. But in a few months, half a year, say, couldn't you..."

She stared at him.

"That is, it happens so rarely. For a mother to want the child back, I mean. Just because you ran into bad luck this time."

"No. I'll never take another, if that's what you're trying to suggest. We hit it off, this baby and me. We had a bond. You don't know what I'm talking about, do you? You don't have any children? Not even married? Well, let me tell you, the bond exists. That is, it does or it doesn't. Sometimes it doesn't, in which case heaven help you, but in this case it did. We had something going, the two of us. I adored her, but she responded to me too, we were a team, a duo, a couple.... Oh, God, why am I saying all this?"

Jay Earling waited a discreet moment. Then in his coaxing, deprecating voice he said there were a few papers they had to go over.

Under his courtly auspices, it went quickly. Another two minutes and she was able to command her voice to tell him that if he would go down in the elevator and outside to the front lawn, the nurse would bring him the child.

It was her firm intention not to watch. Watching that final exit, she told herself, would simply be an exercise in masochistic suffering. Still, when she heard the tread of Claudette's sneakered feet, plus the small protesting chirp of a child taken before it was ready from its crib, when the squeak of the door told her they were gone, she pulled aside the blinds and stationed herself at the window: Linda, the insatiable voyeur.

No packing, they had decreed, but from her perch she could see that under the thin blanket, Claudette had dressed Elena in her jauntiest outfit: a white coverall with red dots that had been a present from the secretaries at the Center during that rhapsodic first week and that just a few days ago turned out to be a perfect fit; and over that a red jacket embroidered with pink and green flowers; and to top it off, this being October, the white bonnet that Linda had bought, one of the indulgences she allowed herself, from the children's store in Mayhew where everything was imported and gorgeous and overpriced.

Her greedy gaze took in all the details: the cautious grasp of Jay Earling's arms as he reached for that not quite acquiescent bundle, and the curve of his back as he leaned forward into the car to work out an arrangement of pillows and safety straps that presumably would keep a child in place, and the quiver of his car as it started, and the despairing look on Claudette's face as at a funereal pace she walked back on the path—she amassed the images into a single picture. This memory of an exit—her keepsake, her souvenir, her momento, like one of the trophies a young child insists on cherishing in a drawer even though the event it commemorates turned out to be a flop.

TWO

"TELL ME, JANEY, how old were you when you started having intercourse?"

She hadn't known till this minute that she would be able to manage. All the way over to the Center, the clear shape of her own dereliction had confronted her. Suppose I break down. Suppose I tell those girls they're no good. Suppose I look at some fifteen-year-old talking about what she does in the back seat of her boyfriend's car and by some subtle shift in my facial expression I let her know she repels me. Worse, suppose I crack. Beaten down by all the prattle of pregnancy and birth and babies, suppose I pull up my skirt like one of those harpies you see in the pictures and yell that Linda Stewart isn't over the hill, as they imagine, that she too has her aches, her urges, her moments of uncontrollable passion.

All rubbish. Of course she was fine. Perhaps more subdued than usual, unwilling to join Louella and Maxine when with shy sympathy they asked her to join them for a coffee break at eleven, but here she is with her first client being neutral, friendly, interested, respectful. Like riding a bicycle. Years may intervene, but still when you get up on it, habit takes you through. Years didn't intervene this time, but trauma did. She's a different person from the woman who sat at this desk yesterday. But look at her, she's doing all right, she can function.

So, then. "Janey, how old were you when you started having intercourse?"

Janey didn't talk loudly—her voice was so soft Linda looked around to make sure the door of her office was closed—but the words were distinct. It was two years ago. She had been thirteen.

"And Janey, can you tell me how you felt about having sex at that age?"

A pause. The girl stroked her earrings, as if those yellow loops were a talisman to impart comfort, and she kept her gaze downward, but the whisper-soft words were forthcoming. Gee, she doesn't know why she did it. She wasn't sure what to do, and you know guys, he wanted it. Another pause. "I was real sorry after. It hurt and I kept thinking about my mother. I just did it. I didn't like it and I did it. I think it's kind of disgusting."

"Well, Janey, what is sex like for you now?"

Stroke, stroke; the earrings trembled. "My boyfriend now is different from the first guy. We don't talk much about it. You know, you're at a party and it just kind of happens."

Janey still didn't look up, so Linda could take a measured look at her. This plaintive little creature to whom, doubtless, life would always just kind of happen.

"What kind of feelings do you have when it just happens?"

"I'm glad he likes me," the whisper said. "Sex, that part of it, that doesn't matter so much. I never ask for it. I guess I don't really like it much. But you can't say no all the time. I try not to think about it."

And after Janey there was Fern, and after her, Theresa. Seeing the last of her morning clients walk out, Linda felt a little quiver of triumph. The worst day of her life, and she had made it through. Habit had clutched her by the back of the neck, so she could handle these girls who slipped into sex without planning for it or wanting it or even especially liking it, who in fact often denied to themselves—*I try not to think about it*—that they had it. There they were, distinct in her book—Janey, ten fifteen; Fern, eleven fifteen; Theresa, twelve—but in her mind they now merged, just as the responses she had made to them merged into one sustaining chord. "So you feel caught in the middle between your mother and your boyfriend," she had at one point—to Fern? to Theresa?—suggested. "You were so good about taking the pills last month, so how do you feel about having forgotten to take them lately?" she had with her friendly voice inquired. "I guess you're feeling really discouraged about your school work," she had proposed. "I hear you saying you don't want to be pregnant"—this surely to Fern—"but you don't feel like having an abortion either," she had tactfully prodded.

All this exploration of feelings. It's what you have to do with these muddled young ones. Not criticize them, not judge them, not falsely sympathize with them, surely not presume to tell them what decisions would be best for them. No. Simply get them to probe honestly till they understand the disheveled feelings that are guiding their behavior so that maybe then they can examine the options and decide on their own what might be best for their lives.

Lucky girls: the thought suddenly struck her. They were in position to make decisions. The options were available to them. All they had to do was reach out and choose. Whereas it was just the opposite for her. In her case, someone else had done the choosing. The door had been shut on the only option she wanted. Without her having any say in the matter, choice had been taken away. Which meant that her feelings were in a different category altogether. Unusable. Useless. Good for no tactical purpose whatever. Any exploring of them on her own part must be maudlin, self-pitying, indulgent, and any expression of them to others could only be gauche and unseemly.

Well, she was in control. She was working on it. In fact, even to Fran, to whom she had talked early this morning, the only time she really let go was when Fran tentatively suggested that she might have acted rather fast. That though it was understandable for Linda not to want to go through the ordeal of a trial, she still didn't have to hand over the baby on the very first day.

"You mean I should have given her a bath last night? Spooned pablum into her? Sat rocking her to sleep? Even though I knew it was the last time? Or the next to last time? Or that maybe with some fancy footwork I could drag the proceedings out for another couple of months? Thanks. Thanks a lot. I guess you're right. I'm too soft. I don't have the stomach for that kind of torment."

Then she saw the stricken look on Fran's face. Unfair, unfair. Fran might be her dear friend and valued colleague, but still you couldn't expect her to come up with adequate consolation. Not at a time when no consolation, however heartfelt or tender, was going to be adequate. Linda opened her pocketbook; in it was a letter from Harold, the man she was going with these days. He had called last night when Claudette was still there, and Claudette had given him the bleak news, and this morning, nice considerate man that he was, he left off this note on his way to his office. He was a dentist, a widower, and he had written a kindly letter, pointed and unique. Well, of course it would have to be unique. There were not many times when one was expected to write a condolence letter covering this particular circumstance. This morning, when Linda stopped for her newspaper at the corner stationery store, she noticed the heading over the display of greeting cards: *Cards for Every Occasion*. A lie. Surely no one had thought to compose a card for the occasion of a woman's having to return a child to its biologic mother.

She put Harold's letter back into her pocketbook. He must have struggled over it inasmuch as its sentiments of regret could not have been entirely sincere. That is, he had been against her adopting a baby in the first place. With the frank egocentricity of a man who relishes his privileges, he suggested that a baby would detract from the attention Linda was able to give him. And in fact the baby had detracted from the attention Linda gave him. So for all his kindness, he would not now welcome an earful about her irremediable loss. Ditto, now she thought about it, for her friends. Indeed, the truth was that none of them had been wholly in favor of the adoption, though they had phrased their reservations in the most oblique of pleasantries. "Just think, when you're fifty years old, to have to be joining a PTA." "You'd better get in shape, hon, to cope with one of those two-year-olds." "At sixty, God help you, you'll be living with an adolescent." Even Fran—supportive, loving Fran—had expressed tactful concern in the shape of admonitions against undue haste.

And maybe they all were right. If something turns out badly, isn't that sufficient reason for judging it to have been a mistake? By that token, the adoption of Elena had indeed been a big mistake.

The second big mistake of her life. The first was not having had her own child fifteen years ago. She could have. The opportunity was available. The invitation was offered. It came from Ted, when they were in their third year of what was turning out to be a rocky marriage. Fights, threats, reconciliations, fights, threats, more and more feeble reconciliations. "Maybe it would help if we had a child," he said to her one night. It was after one of their most savage quarrels. They had said inexcusable, unforgettable things to each other. He taunted her with being prissy, the most unattractive kind of prig, because she ascribed to his affairs such a feverish importance. Was she really set on a degree in psychology? Planning to make a career of working with people? What a bust she would be, someone with so little tolerance and understanding. God help the person who would come to her expecting help while confessing to some transitory weakness.

She countered that his sexual exploits were simply a matter of seeking power. When he took a woman to bed, it was so he could get the better of her, impose his will on her. He was unable to attach himself to one person: afraid of being emotionally dependent. It was a sign of his essential narcissism that he craved emotional titillation but couldn't accept honest involvement. She felt uplifted saying these things. Classic arguments. Arguments out of the textbooks that as a graduate student she was beginning to study.

When they both subsided into a sheepish breathlessness, he made the remark. "Maybe it would help if we had a child." She stared; what in God's name was he talking about? "Linda, come on. You know. A baby. Our baby. Just possibly it would do us good." She looked at his face, crunched up in fatuous earnestness, and she didn't stop to think; the words flew out in a rush. "That's a disgusting idea. Cheap, vulgar, disgusting. Like people who decide to build a house when they can't get it together, they think that great house is going to solve their problems. If we can't make it now, we should impose a rotten marriage on an innocent child."

Innocent. Rotten. Disgusting. Cheap. Satisfying, simplistic words. Words to match the principles she then held sacred. Now she thought of that vehement refusal. If she'd gone ahead and done what Ted suggested, the girl—of course it would have been a girl— would be fourteen. Linda would be a forty-two year-old woman with a fourteen-year-old daughter. Everything seemly, orderly, regularized. Her life fulfilled. Her path sweetly, irrevocably laid out.

Sometimes Linda allowed herself to picture the girl. A door opening, an unobtrusive sound, a furtive cough, and the image would be there before her. A bright girl, with Ted's uncontrollably curly hair but Linda's fair coloring and small bones and calm, even features. She would be wearing the standard adolescent accouterments—the patched jeans, the run-down sneakers, the books balanced on one hip—but from the inquiring gaze, something fresh and spirited would shine out. Even when she came with the most ordinary of requests—"Mom, you have to sign this paper so I can go on the class trip"—you would note the sweetness, the intelligence.

The door opened now; Fran came in. Fran wearing on her long scrubbed face a very different expression from her morning one of fervent sympathy. And plunging, as she stood in front of the desk, into an inquiry that was not ordinary at all. "Linda, what was the baby wearing?"

"Wearing?"

"When you . . . that is, when Jay Earling took her."

"Claudette dressed her." Why didn't she give a straight answer, what was there about Fran's face to impel this evasion?

"Right. So what did Claudette put on."

"That white coverall with red dots, you remember, Debbie and Felice gave it to me when we had that shower but it was too big until just last week. And a red jacket embroidered with pink and green flowers and her white—Fran, what is it?"

"Linda, I'm sorry. Oh, God, this is terrible. Thing is, they're both dead. Both of them. Marylou and the baby. Drowned. No, someone killed Marylou first. Strangled her. I guess she was holding the child, and then he...they...whoever...threw both of them into that river, no a pond, they call it Hommocks Pond, this place in Mayhew, and this morning, when some boys were playing . . . Linda! Linda, dear, please!"

THREE

LATER SHE THOUGHT she must have expected to get the baby back. Under her disarray, her stony demeanor, her try at stoicism in front of Jay Earling, that subversive idea must have been working all along: Marylou would find the care of a child too burdensome or unsettling or confining or just plain boring; she would admit her mistake and the process of official transfer would begin again the other way. Yes, that was the idea she must have cherished in her mind. Otherwise why would she now be so stricken with grief? A second grieving, and in a sense an impermissible one, because she had so strongly avowed that the child had died to her when it was returned to Marylou.

When she thought this, she was at the police station, talking to an officer named Wilkerson. He was in charge of the investigation, and by the time she arrived, he knew about her part in the baby's abbreviated life. He had heard it from Jay Earling and, in a more limited way, also from Marylou's father, whose name was Will Rogin. Wilkerson was a considerate man as well, she guessed, as an efficient one, and as she sat in his office he bothered her with the minimum of questions before telling her what both these men had told him.

Earling, it seemed, brought the child to Marylou at about two o'clock; half an hour, that is, after leaving Linda. Afternoon traffic was heavy in the two villages he had to go through, which troubled him because he didn't have a real baby seat in his car, just a makeshift enclosure he had constructed out of straps and pillows. Besides, the baby was crying, so he was glad to hand it over. Marylou lived in the last house on a block of small two-family houses, and he went inside to attend, once again, to the ritual signing of forms. Did Marylou display any special emotion? Not so that he noticed. She handled the child gingerly, not with any special show of affection but not with carelessness either. She laid it on the couch and pushed a chair in front so the child would not roll off. No, he didn't see any signs of equipment around, but not being a family man, he was not sure what equipment to look for. Besides, since the bedrooms were in back, he guessed this was where she'd have put a crib or a carriage or whatever. And no, she did not let slip any hint about where she was going next or whom she might be planning to see. Nor did she express any gratitude for the lawyer's efforts on her behalf, but maybe he'd been wrong to expect it. After all, adolescents.

As for Marylou's father, his testimony was even less help. He had not known Marylou was getting the baby back. She had not consulted him. Consult! What was he saying. She hadn't even bothered to tell him.

Hadn't let her own father in on a decision so momen-
tous. That was Marylou for you. High-handed, reckless. She was dead now, poor girl, but he had to say
she had a will of her own. Ever since her mother died
when she was twelve, it had been like that. Obstinacy,
thoughtlessness, folly—some would come out and call
it downright disobedience. For instance, one summer
she had got a job at Norwell's. Little notion store on
Main Street—Wilkerson must know it. One of those
places where a customer buys a single spool of thread
for seventy cents and leaves on the counter ten things
she decides she doesn't want. It was Marylou's job to
put them back—not bad work for a fifteen-year-old
girl, which she was then. In fact, he'd been instru-
mental in getting it for her. He did some renovation for
them—he was a self-employed carpenter. And you
better believe he had a time convincing Mr. Norwell he
could rely on Marylou. So what happens? Just before
she's due to start she announces that she's leaving next
morning to be a chambermaid at a motel out on the
Island. Not at all the kind of place where he wants her
to be. That's Marylou all over. Acting up on her own.
No thought for him, her father, how it's going to make
him look.

And, of course, having that baby in the first place.
Did she ask what he thought of it? Did she even tell
him she was pregnant till it was too late to do anything about it? With no sense of decency, she just went
ahead, day after day taking her big belly into those
high school classrooms. And not even a regular ma-

NO DURESS 43

ternity dress. No. Just those shameless sweaters, stretched out in front. Really, it made him ill to see her.

Linda was silent a long minute after Wilkerson's voice wound down. "He doesn't sound like the most loving father."

"Well, love," Wilkerson judiciously said. "In his book, love means control. A daughter toes the line. Asks your permission. Says, Whatever you think best, Daddy."

"I guess he hasn't been around much these days."

"A man alone, don't forget. A man alone with a difficult adolescent. Some fathers could handle it. This one obviously couldn't." Outside, there was a small commotion: two young men walking by in handcuffs. Wilkerson said something to the policeman escorting them—then he closed the door. "In a way you can see Mr. Rogin's point. There they are in the same house, eating at the same table, breaking the same bread. And he's in the dark. He's not part of her life. He has no idea what his only child is up to." Wilkerson's sigh might or might not indicate a sense of male partisanship. "So if the girl was involved in something, some drug business, say, we can't hope to find out about it from him."

Linda looked over Wilkerson's head, where the posters were hung end to end. *We Are Looking for the Finest—A Career with Benefits* covered one corner of *If You Can't Tell Anyone, Tell Us—Incest Hotline.* "Are you suggesting that Marylou was involved in some drug business? That you know about it?"

There was a pile of No Parking signs on his desk—
No Parking Saturday, Eight to Two, black letters on
yellow cardboard—and Wilkerson straightened it.
"On the plea, the fevered plea, I might say, of Mr.
Oliver, who's the principal over at Plains High School,
we've been keeping an eye on a particular bunch. One
of them—a boy in her class—lives around the corner
from Marylou. He was arrested twice last summer,
and twice, through some loophole or other, he got off.
A couple of times these past weeks he's been seen giving Marylou a ride home from school in his expensive
sports car." Wilkerson laid his hands on the desk, as
if in a demonstration of essential emptiness. "Those
are all the facts we have. So is Mr. Oliver correct in his
suspicions? Is there really a gang peddling drugs at
Plains High School? If there is, was Marylou involved in it? If she was involved, did she turn on them
or threaten to do something so they'd find it expedient to kill her? At this point, Miss Stewart, you can fill
in the answers as well as we can."

"What about the lawyer? Jay Earling. Inciden-
tally, how did you know to call him?"

"We found one of his business cards in her wallet.
Her water-soaked wallet," he flatly added.

"Well, do you trust Earling?" she said. "All that
about his driving to her house and leaving the baby
and no hint of what she was up to—do you believe
it?"

"Miss Stewart, do you know any reason why we
shouldn't?"

In her keyed-up state, everything unnerved her. The regretful monotone in which he spoke. The contrast between the quiet here in his small office and the clatter outside: people shuffling by, bells ringing, sirens down in the parking lot. Even those cluttered decorations, none of the posters exactly aligned.

Or maybe it was Lieutenant Wilkerson himself. Maybe comfort would have flowed more readily from a different kind of policeman. Someone all crassness and distrust, out of hard-boiled tradition. Someone to say, I suspect you all. You and you and you, you too, Miss Stewart. Someone, indeed, whose very brutishness would appear to promise vigilant searches, secret sources, wild chases through the night. Anyone but this considerate Wilkerson with his air of murky sympathy, his implication that when it came to discovering what had happened, she was in partnership with him.

He was waiting: any reason not to trust Jay Earling? She saw the man leaning against her fireplace mantel: the springy gait, the boyish shine, the hair tossed back from the high forehead. "Of course I'm not accusing Jay Earling. Is there a gracious way to take off someone's child? Do the books of etiquette prescribe a nice way to handle it? All I know is, he had a nasty job to do and he did it. Naturally I don't exactly love him for having carried off my baby, but once Marylou got him back in the case, I don't see what else he could have done."

"But you do think somebody was in there with a scheme?"

"It's like you and that drug business," she burst out. "Obviously, I don't have anything definite. But there's a big market in babies these days, I'm surely not telling you anything new. Plenty of people, plenty right here in this County, would gladly pay the earth for a healthy white five-month-old child."

"So you're suggesting that someone induced, or let's say bribed, Marylou to pretend she wanted the baby for herself, but she was really supposed to hand it over so then that person could sell it?"

She doesn't want to be in partnership with this policeman. She doesn't even want to be in his confidence. She wants to go home and curl up in bed and have him call tomorrow morning to say they have it all solved. She kept her gaze on another poster. *Have You Been the Victim of a Crime? Call Crime Victims' Board*. "It's Marylou herself. When you think about it, she didn't act like any innocent."

"In what way?"

"When she came to my office yesterday, I didn't stop to analyze what she was saying. I was frantic. I lost my head. All that got through was that she was taking back my baby. But now I think about it, some very curious business."

"Such as what?"

For a second she couldn't speak. Trying to reconstruct that conversation brought back the pain that had been part of it. "She talked about an extended

family. The extended family she and this other girl
with a baby would make up. Well, extended family.
It's sociologists' lingo. It's not the kind of phrase your
average high school senior is in the habit of tossing
around.''

"Anything else?"

"She knew about some testimony I'd given in a
custody case. It was between adoptive parents and a
birth mother—a case, that is, sort of like hers and
mine. She didn't just know. She had the words written down, she threw my own quotes back at me. But
that case was two years ago. Two years ago she was
fifteen. Not exactly the age when you're reading the
law journals. Not even, probably, local newspapers.''

Wilkerson said nothing.

"And then all that about my having coerced her.
First of all, I didn't. She got all the requisite counseling from the Center. They were very careful. They
made sure she understood her rights. But even if I had,
how'd she know to bring it up? Coercion: that classic
weapon in custody battles, that word that goes right
to a judge's sanctimonious heart. So who indoctrinated her? Who wised her up? Who primed her in the
most effective tactic to use against me?''

"What was Marylou like when she came to see
you?"

The pain had not gone away. "She seemed to have
gotten more mature. At least she said she was more
mature. She said she'd done a lot of serious thinking,
and like an idiot I believed her.''

"Maybe she was telling the truth," Wilkerson said. "That's just as reasonable. She decided she wanted the baby back, and she went to people who gave her some good advice. That testimony of yours—am I right in thinking it was publicized at the time? That lots of people knew about it? So isn't it possible that one of them sympathized with her and put her on to those devastating quotes?"

That dry reproachful voice, when the conviction of treachery was rising within her. "There's only one thing that sounds reasonable to me. Someone is placing babies illegally, and that person knew of a particular baby who might be available, and he or she cleverly groomed Marylou to get hold of it."

Wilkerson's phone rang. He looked at it, but he didn't pick it up. Then he granted her a brief smile, a smile of official tolerance. That theory had a lot going for it, he said. "But I'm afraid it won't wash, Miss Stewart. In the kind of episode you're talking about, a child's the prize, the booty, the treasure. Maybe you kill the mother because she changes her mind or threatens to talk or otherwise looks like making trouble. But you guard the child. You take impeccable care of the child. You keep it safe. You surely don't throw it into a body of water where someone may or may not come along to find it by morning.... Miss Stewart, I'm sorry to have offended you."

It was a baby who had been offended. A baby fished up from that muddy pond—that was the offense she would never get over. They had asked if she wanted to see the baby when she came in; all things considered, her right. She shook her head. No. Thanks, but no. It was enough to imagine what could happen to that rosy body after twelve hours in stagnant water. But she did look, at their request, at the clothes, which Wilkerson had in a bag. Baby clothes, made of materials meant to be washed often; those hours of immersion had hardly impaired them. Still the dashing red dots on the white coverall, the embroidered flowers on the diminutive red jacket, the strings dangling from the bonnet. Only the bonnet looked ruined—she put out her hand to test that lost crispness and then drew it back.

As if to erase that bedraggled sight from her mind, she fixed her gaze on still another of the posters. *Picnic Sunday, November 11, at Hommocks Field. Benefit Patrolmen's Benevolent Association.* "Hommocks. Isn't that where it happened?"

He said the field was indeed adjacent to the pond.

"That pond. What's it like?"

"Sort of a desolate place. It's County land, no special beauty or other attractions. The creek that runs down Rawley Road feeds into it. Some call it a pond, some say lake. In winter, if the weather hits right, a cold spell and no snow, there can be ice skating. On the other, the north side, there's a footpath. The Mayhew Garden Club tried to make it into a nature trail some years back. They put up a few signs, labeled the trees, but in the end it came to nothing. And sometimes the boys try fishing. That's what was go-

ing on this morning. Boys playing hooky, going fishing.''

"That's how they found it?"

That was how.

"That place—pond, lake, whatever. It doesn't
sound like the kind of place a girl like Marylou would
be likely to hang out."

Something else they didn't know, he admitted. Had
she been killed there? Or was she killed someplace else
and taken there? If someone had been trying to hide a
body, a pond that was generally deserted may have
seemed a good idea. On the other hand, for someone
driving up in a car, the water was not especially easy
to get to.

"Not accessible at all," Wilkerson drearily in-
sisted. "From where you park the car, you have to
walk across maybe thirty feet of rocks and mud. There
are clumps of bushes near the road. If someone's lug-
ging a body and wants to hide it, those bushes, I
should think, would serve the purpose even better. So
why the water? Why stumble across all that rocky ter-
rain to get to the water? What's the advantage? As I
say"—that gesture with his empty hands, denoting
chumminess and ignorance both—"your guess is as
good as mine."

She didn't answer. But she thought his guess might
be, considering his position should be, a lot better than
hers. And she saw no benefit in being in his confidence when that meant both of them were in the dark.

FOUR

"THEY DON'T KNOW a damn thing." When she went to the front of the police station where Fran was waiting, she felt Fran's hand lightly on her shoulder, guiding her toward the parking lot. The warily protective touch you reserve for invalids or children or mourners. "That Wilkerson. He seems intelligent and he obviously knows his way around adolescents—well, a police officer in this town, how could he not? But under all the snappy talk, there's a big nothing. Why was she dumped in a pond, for God's sake? What was she doing with a baby in that unlikely place? Did someone kill her somewhere else and bring her there? What was the reason for killing her? He doesn't know. He doesn't pretend to know."

"No leads at all?" Fran drove cautiously, as though transporting something fragile.

"Just the usual slippery ones. High school kids these days can be a troublesome lot. The high school principal has been conferring with the police about some choice troublemakers who may be into selling drugs. One of them lives around the corner from Marylou. Last week he drove her home. Maybe that's the reason she was killed. Maybe not." She put her head back on the headrest. "You know what? I guess it proves something bitchy about me, but I can't concentrate on Marylou. Oh, I'm sorry she was killed, a young girl, it's terrible. But what beats me, why did someone kill that baby? From where I'm sitting, there was no excuse. None. A baby can't tell tales. It can't pick someone out of a lineup. It can't say, This tall guy with red hair and a moustache, he was the one who drove the car. The murderer could have taken the baby someplace. The steps of a church. The front door of a house. Or even, if they were afraid of being seen, just left it there. On a rock. Under a tree. It wasn't so cold last night, she could have lived. There are stories of babies who survive for days. Throwing that child in after Marylou, that's what I—Fran, where are you going?''

"Taking you home."

Home where the crib was still against the wall of a pink painted room, the clothes were folded inside the three small drawers of a dresser, the carriage obstructed the hall between kitchen and bathroom. She couldn't face them, but she couldn't bring herself to get rid of them either.

"Why should I go home? I have appointments at work, don't I? Besides," she said coldly, "people should be able to work no matter what personal misfortune—Fran? Fran darling. I'm sorry."

From time to time, there was a day when Fran didn't show up for work. Migraine, she would abstractedly say. Everyone knew it was her husband. Her husband who after twenty years of marriage was dying of melanoma. "I didn't even stay home with him the whole time," she said to Linda after one of those days. "You know what I did? Went to the movies. A double feature. Four hours. Then I fell asleep and sat another hour. The new medicine isn't working, I couldn't face him, but I couldn't bear hearing the problems of some skittish sixteen-year-old either."

"Oh, Fran. I guess we both have to bumble through."

"How about tonight? That should take plenty of bumbling."

"Tonight?"

"Linda, the annual dinner. Did you forget?"

She sat forward so abruptly her head bumped the dashboard. "You don't really think I'm going to a dinner tonight. Get dressed in my spiffy best and sit smiling through all that hoopla. Tonight!"

For a second, Fran didn't answer. Though a woman on the curb had no intention of crossing, Fran put on the brake and waited. "Linda, dear, listen. It'll be terrible for you, I know. Ghastly. But you're part of the reason the dinner is held. The donors expect you. The trustees do. The Friends of the Center do. They don't know what's going on with your life and I don't think you especially want them to. They just know Linda Stewart, senior counselor, should be at her assigned table. All that fancy food and the snazzy hotel—they pretend they're doing us a favor, but it's their chance to check us out. See have we sprouted two heads during the year."

"Anyhow, they'll probably cancel the dinner. A girl serviced by the Center found murdered—they won't go ahead with it."

This time Fran didn't wait at all. "Linda, you have to be kidding. Just because a girl was killed? Because out of the hundreds of girls we service each year, one was found killed?" Fran turned the corner to the Center. "Remember two years ago? There was that hideous accident, half a dozen drunk high school kids smashing into a truck, four killed, one paralyzed, and still the dinner went ahead. Someone simply used it to underline the theme of his speech. Just shows how important it is to support an institution like the Center, so we can work to prevent such grievous occurrences. All that smarmy piety," her brisk voice said as she maneuvered into a parking space. "Someone will refer to Marylou, he'll say what a tragedy, what trouble those confused young ones can get into, we'll just have to redouble our efforts."

Fran had it right. Marylou was mentioned in every speech. Not by name. She was that Very Sad Happening, that Terrible Incident, that Tragic Headline, the Reminder For All Of Us. Everyone also said an incident like that justified our working still harder to reach out to these young people, that's why we're so grateful to the dedicated staff. No one made particular mention of the baby, but as Fran had predicted, no one at the speakers' table knew that the baby had more than a tangential interest for one of the members of the staff; as far as they were concerned, a drowned baby was just another detail to make the incident sad, grim, tragic, capable of pointing a moral.

But of course the people at Linda's table knew. At her table were Fran and Maxine, another counselor, and Roy Gardiner, the doctor who worked at the Center two afternoons a week, and Debbie Fine and Felice Arkin, the two secretaries, and Louella Case, the OB nurse; and all of them, at one time or other during the evening, told Linda that under the circumstances she was great, foolish, gutsy, an example of superhuman control to sit here. They also, in their kindly way, offered to cover for her if she decided to leave. She was longing to leave. She disliked these affairs, who didn't. Such bootlicking. Such servile compliments. Such wheedling requests couched in terms of fatuous compliments. And in her head, as the evening progressed, such a sense of outrage. For professionals like Fran and Maxine and herself to be able to conduct their work only if people with too much money like the Van Cleavers and the Stanhopes and the Shaws were persuaded to shell out some small portion of it in their direction. But she stayed, of course—walking out was not to be considered—and presently, as always happened, the outrage turned to indifference and then to a wry kind of curiosity. Would the main speaker overemphasize adolescent sexuality to get the attention of donors, and also turn them off by conjuring up images of promiscuity? Would he leave his audience thinking the guidance sessions were really methods courses? Would he end

up making those touchy listeners feel punitive instead
of supportive? And also—no small matter—would he
be able to attain this year, as speakers sometimes but
not always attained in other years, a sensible balance
between adulation and substance?

The main speaker tonight was a Professor Moss,
who was director of the Department of Health Services at a noted university, and also past president of
the Gedney Family Planning Center, and he was edg-
ing into substance now. "Let me tell you what happened to me the other day. A girl came into my office
and said, 'A friend has a problem.' Well, we all know
what that means, and after a few minutes, Marcy
made the standard admission. I told her where to go
for a pregnancy test, and we made another appointment." His head swiveled, giving the nod to both sides
of the room, which was in Riverview's largest hotel; he
had a commanding presence and a facile delivery.
"When the test came back positive, we sat down,
Marcy and I, and had a good discussion about what
she should do. We even wrote out the options, all the
pros and cons. All very sound and orderly. She decided to have an abortion, and I gave her a referral and
also another appointment for some weeks hence."

Professor Moss waited. Going through the swing-
ing doors at the rear, one of the waiters had dropped
a tray. Some speedy repair work—this hotel knew how
to handle crises—and his deep voice continued.
"Three days later, Marcy was back. 'A friend of mine
has a problem,' she said. Aha. Then, only then, I re-

alized. The only way Marcy could cope with her feelings about being pregnant was by denying her pregnancy. In our earlier session, I hadn't explored those feelings. I had simply explained to her the mechanical things to do about pregnancy. In short, I was supporting an unproductive coping pattern. Under my tutelage, this mixed-up and troubled young girl wasn't really deciding things. She was playing at pseudo-decision making."

Another pause. The head swiveled to the left, where the two staff tables were placed. "That's where the Center's able staff comes in. They know that for the confused Marcys, it is vital not simply to learn the facts, but to be able to integrate what they learn. These counselors have mastered the tactics for accomplishing this. They're pros at reproductive health care counseling, and I'm proud to be able to appear with them tonight."

Linda drew her fork through the mound of mashed potatoes on her plate. She knew the story about Marcy. It was a generic story. They all told it. Sometimes the girl was Lillian, sometimes Faith, sometimes Claire. But it won the audience, which after all was its purpose. "When I came in this evening, I was told of the dreadful occurrence regarding a girl in this community," Professor Moss went soberly on. "All I can say is, such an incident can only underline for us the dangers facing these young people, and the great importance of our professional intercession. So go to it, all you workers at the Center. My hat is off to you," he resoundingly finished, and Linda saw nods from the heavy-set woman next to him who must be his wife, and from Sig and Judy Shaw, whose money came from cosmetics, and from Annette Van Cleaver, who had inherited her money, and also from the remarkably pretty woman in pink satin next to her, whom Linda had never seen before.

She leaned past the centerpiece of yellow and blue flowers so she could stare at this phenomenon. Everyone dressed to the teeth for these occasions; while avowing their reluctance, they still sported their finery. Even Maxine changed from her determined costume of man-tailored suits and austere blouses; even Louella took off the nurse's uniform that she wore as a badge of honor. But among all the neat dresses and silk blouses, who else would go in for pink satin with a low-cut neckline? Who else, for that matter, would have such a heavenly bosom for the low-cut neckline to bare, or such a delectable face to rise above it.

Next to the vision in pink, a trustee now rose to glide over some figures. A fund bigger than... a list of clients five percent ahead of... a staff with more degrees than... his voice lightly stroked through the felicitous items. Considering all this, he said—they were clearing the dishes with their piles of chicken bones by this time—considering these milestones, he wished to express some specific gratitude. To Dr. Roy Gardiner, that distinguished practitioner. To Frances Low and Linda Stewart and Maxine Hammond, without whose expert and compassionate services. To

Debbie Fine and Felice Arkin, on whose dogged loy-
alty we all. To Louella Case and Madge Boyer, our
excellent nurses. Finally, special thanks to Jay Earling, who makes sure the affairs of the Center continue on an even legal keel.

Linda looked up. Of course Jay Earling; how could
she forget. There he was at the table next to the head
one, the boyish shine suffused with pleasure. Then the
pleasure turned to something sharper, a gratification
he shared with others, as she heard the master of cer-
emonies say, "And now my great privilege to present
Mrs. Rosalie Stanhope." At which, with an affecting
little shrug, as if to wonder why they should bother
with her at all, the vision in pink stood up.

She was even better standing. You saw not just the
heart-shaped face, the wide-set eyes, the dark curly
hair, but the slope of sugary shoulders, the hands
clasping and unclasping, the belt that cinched in a
minuscule waist. Jay Earling wasn't the only one staring. When Linda looked around, she saw the acclaim
from all of them. Stunned attention.

And the woman's voice didn't turn them off. That
thin, faintly nasal, slightly slurred voice—they looked
tolerant. Even Fran, her chin resting amiably on her
palm as if to say, Well, poor sweet darling, you can't
expect her to be perfect.

Oh, no. Not perfect at all. Rosalie Stanhope didn't
trust herself to speak her speech freely. Not the greeting: "It gives me great pleasure to be here tonight."
Not the acknowledgment: "Such an honor to be con-

nected with your splendid institution." And surely not the reason for her presence: "As you probably know, I'm here because my husband Claude couldn't make it." No. None of that delivered with eyes fixed on the audience. All of it, rather, read out from the pieces of paper she held unabashed in her hand and laid aside as each was finished.

"Claude had every intention of being here. I'm sure you all hoped he would be here. Until two days ago, I certainly expected him to be here. But those expeditions are so dependent on the weather. And when the weather in that brutal place turned bad last week, the men realized they would have to stay longer to finish all their measurements."

Measurements: she put down a piece of paper and the audience relapsed into indulgent smiles. They had all read in the local papers about Claude Stanhope, who was not just one of the largest donors to the Center, but one of the authentic celebrities of the County. It had been worth a column a year and a half ago when the eminent scientist Claude Stanhope married a woman twenty-nine years younger than he was; it merited almost as much space when the happy couple bought an estate (see picture above) in Mayhew Gardens; and six months ago it had rated a half page in the Sunday section when a reporter wrangled from Dr. Stanhope an interview about his forthcoming expedition to the Arctic Circle. The nature of the arcane tests being undertaken in that remote area was not fully explained, but you understood that they were for the public good, and well worth the staggering effort of the trip itself.

His wife, in fact, was saying it. "Claude would not be up there if he didn't feel so deeply about the stake of all of us in the scientific results. And I can't say it the way he would, but he'd surely want me to say what a wonderful job you people do at the Center. He'd feel it even more now that he's a father himself. I remember his face that morning he left. Our baby was just six days old, and as he bent over the crib his eyes filled with tears because he would be missing those thrilling first months. He was so proud of that child. He considered her so beautiful—well, she is a little beauty. He expected such great things of her. So if he knew about the tragedy that we heard on the radio today, if he knew what happened to a child who was just about the same age as ours, he would say it's even more important for the Center to continue its fine work. To reach those troubled teenagers and help them make the right choices."

Rosalie Stanhope looked up. End of sentence—indeed, to her gratified surprise, end of speech—so she could put the last page down and give them all the benefit of her lovely smile. Starry-eyed complacence.

Linda clapped like everyone else. Clapped despite the heartache. It's not fair. Birdbrain like that can have a baby, and mine is taken from me. Then she leaned back. Was she going to be like this, grudging every other woman her share of happiness? Yes, for a while she would be like this. Rancorous. Mean-spirited. Resentful. A resentment augmented tonight by the tribute to Rosalie Stanhope's beauty.

Then it appeared the tribune was not unanimous after all. "Tramp," a voice said clearly behind her back. Linda turned. At the table beside theirs, too close to theirs, really, a woman sat hunched over, mumbling into her chin. "No-good tramp," she said again.

"I beg your pardon?"

"Rosie up there. Little lying no-good tramp. I ought to know." The woman was not as old as she first appeared. Despite the gray in the wiry hair hanging low over her forehead, and the intimidating bust under a navy suit, the hands writhing in her lap were smooth, unspotted.

Linda leaned toward her. What do you know that you call her a tramp? The words were on her tongue. But at the last instant she drew back. You had to watch it. You particularly had to watch it if you got your living from the Center. As Fran had pointed out, this whole glossy show—the black tie waiters and the plentiful supply of wine and the flashily presented food—was for them. Linda, Maxine, Louella—all of them. To salute their work but also to appraise it. She had peered past the lush centerpiece to turn her critical gaze on Rosalie Stanhope, but you never knew what criticism might be going in the opposite direction. At a dinner contrived to butter up the Center donors, a Center staff person had better not give the impression of allying herself with the wrong company.

She straightened her chair and stared down at the sherbet—three different colors—melting on her plate. She hadn't wanted to come tonight, God knows she hadn't wanted to come; only Fran's sane counsel had persuaded her. But somehow, though the pain was as severe, she felt stronger. Or at least less numb. She thought of the smug distress with which people had greeted each mention of the day's Terrible Tragedy, especially she thought of Rosalie Stanhope reading from the script about her own beautiful child, and something decisive stirred within her; anger imparted fortitude. Her hands dutifully clapped for some final speaker up there on the platform while her mind affirmed that whoever had killed that baby had not heard the last from the baby's true mother.

FIVE

"THEY HAVEN'T HEARD the last from me," she told Fran. It was next morning; they were having coffee in Fran's office before anyone should come in.

"Linda, now what?"

"I want to know why that baby had to be killed."

"Last night upset you, didn't it?"

Upset! Is that what she was? When she went home with the words about another woman's child ringing in her ears, could "upset" cover it? Could it possibly?

She took a sleeping pill before she went to bed, but it didn't help. As she lay with her eyes closed, the face of her own child was before her. Elena didn't respond like other babies—first a doubtful half smile, then the lips tentatively widening, then the standard cheery salute. No. She kept back the smile, withheld it—a sweet tease—until it was clear the occasion really warranted it. Then eyes and mouth and cheeks all broke out into radiance. Beatific joy. With the bare feet, as often as not, wriggling in accompaniment and the hands quivering in appreciative motion.

Linda picked up her coffee cup. She said sure, she'd been upset, but in fact the dinner turned out no better or worse than usual, and it didn't affect what she was saying.

"Linda, why don't you let it alone? Nosing around, asking questions—is that what you have in mind? You together with the police? No? Christ, you independent of the police? You'll hate it. You'll come up against hostility and outrage and apprehension. If you're official, it's one thing. But Linda Stewart playing detective—ask a question and right away it's pejorative. So why, Linda? Why?"

"I owe it to the baby." She didn't have to look at Fran's briefly wincing face to hear the pompous note in her words. At the same time, she didn't disavow their sentiment.

Fran took another muffin. When her husband's illness was first diagnosed, she said that the one good thing about her kind of anguish was that you stopped eating. Now she could get rid of that excess fat. But it worked the other way. Anxiety stimulated appetite: at lunch, she was the one to tell the waitress she'd have the layered chocolate cake for dessert, and if you looked into her trash basket, you saw the candy wrappers mixed in with the crumpled papers. These months at the end simply hastened the process. Linda knew that under Fran's blouse, a safety pin held together the two ends of skirt that she could no longer close.

"Linda, you must have some ideas or you wouldn't—"

"Okay. My ideas. I don't buy that business of a drug gang. I know in the world of today's high schools it makes sense, and in the end maybe the police will come up with the proof. But right now? Uh uh. I think something to do with us. The Center. The Center and possibly the New Beginnings Adoption Agency we sometimes work with. You got it, Fran. The black market in babies we know perfectly well is prevalent as weeds." She crushed her paper cup and threw it away. "So the big question: if there is this black market, who's abetting it? Who knows about what babies are being born and is capitalizing on that knowledge? Around here it could be anyone. You, me, Maxine, Roy Gardiner, Louella, Debbie, Jay Earling... anyone. Everyone." She watched Fran put down a muffin and on second thought pick it up.

"What about Jay Earling?"

"It's what Wilkerson asked me. I told him the truth. Naturally I hate the man—his were the arms that carried my baby off. But do I think he killed Marylou? No on two counts. One, if there is this scheme, killing the baby was an accident. A bizarre, clumsy accident. Out there on those chilly rocks, someone made some inept moves. And I don't see Jay Earling in that scenario. He isn't the accident type. Not him. He's sharp and he's also agile. I saw the way he handled the child at my house, watching his step every inch of the way. No heart, maybe, but clever hands." She put sugar into her second cup and then remembered she had put it in already.

"I can't even see him carrying a body over to the water. I drove over there yesterday—yes, Fran, I went to look at it. Like Wilkerson said, it's a haul from the road to the pond. A tough haul over rocks, and Jay's slight, and Marylou, you saw her chunky figure. The natural, the practical thing would've been to stow a body—Wilkerson said this too—under some clumps of bushes. And Jay, from what I've seen of him, is nothing if not practical. So who did it? Who's our clumsy and impractical murderer?"

She saw the tight-lipped look on Fran's face—the look that said, You're getting in over your head—but Fran simply asked if there was anything she could do to help.

"Actually, there is. If any other girls from Plains High School come in, I want them referred to me. My clients. Don't worry, I'll do everything right by them. But if they let slip anything about being paid money for having a baby, or if they have a line on Marylou, if they even knew Marylou, I'll be the one to hear it. Only not today," she went on quickly. "Today I'm checking out of here. Going to see people. Do I expect some great revelations? Do I think anyone will tell me the truth? Do I even know if they'll see me? No to all of that."

No also to much more speculation. Phones were ringing, people talking, footsteps sounding outside in the hall. If she wanted to get out, she had to do it fast. "Who's on my list? First Lee Hevessy, who runs New Beginnings, which is by all odds the best adoption

agency in this neck of the woods. And then Jay Earling, and then Marylou's father."

"I can understand Hevessy, I can even figure the
father. But Jay—I thought you crossed him off."

"No one is crossed off." She knew Fran was looking at her. Such inconsistency. Such ambivalence.
Such swings from yes to no. "Besides, I thought of a
neat way to get at him," she went on. "No questions.
Just a sidelong approach. One that could conceivably
trap him if he is involved. Fran, darling, wish me
luck."

Lee Hevessy would see her, indeed canceled an appointment to see her. And at first she said all the right
things. "Oh, my dear, I'm so sorry. What can I say?
It's a heartbreak. To have a child and lose it—it's the
worst. It's enough to make you lose faith." She was a
thin woman, almost as tall as Linda, and her angular
face looked sharper by reason of the graying hair that
was cut straight across her forehead and then hung
down severely on either side. But her voice was warm
and soft, the kind of voice that soothes you with its
practiced calm.

She also knew how to sit silent while Linda explained her visit in the same terms she'd used for Fran.
Too few white babies...possibilities for corrup-
tion...Marylou obviously indoctrinated by someone
in the know...of course she doesn't think the New
Beginnings Agency...

"But you do think it. In your heart it's what you
think." The warm voice could modulate, it seemed,

into accents of sudden rancor. "This respectable agency, but it's not all peachy clean. It can't be, considering the nature of our work. There's a rake-off—you really think it. Why shouldn't you? Everyone thinks it. The people we serve, the ones we turn down, the judges, the public, everyone. We get our cut. A few of us anyhow. We have it made."

"Lee, listen—"

"You know where I live? On the left side of a two-family house on Grant Street. My landlord is an electrician; he has his office on the other side. His customers come at all hours—sometimes they ring his bell, sometimes they ring mine. The backyard is full of his cast-offs, so I have a window box outside my kitchen window. That's my garden—a three-foot window box." She laid her hands flat on the desk. "In this classy suburb, where you expect a swimming pool and tennis court with every house, I have room to grow six geraniums."

"Lee, will you please shut up? I don't think any of that. About your being a cheat. I lost my baby; that's why I'm here. I lost her and no one has any clues and I'm desperate."

They both sat silent a second. Then Lee Hevessy sighed. "Linda, I'm sorry. You're one of those underpaid workers too, don't I know it. I just get so sick of it. All these filthy-rich people, and that's how they console themselves. Thinking we get our share. Our cut under the table."

It was what Fran had warned her. Ask a question, and right away it's pejorative.

"Besides, if you think that girl, what's her name, the birth mother, if she was taking money for someone who wanted a baby, why would the baby be drowned?"

The maddening question. Did she suppose she could avoid it this time? "You know what? I don't think the plan was to murder anyone. I think it was just to be the standard order of business. A little money for Marylou, a lot for the intermediaries, a child for some couple who could shell out plenty. Only something went wrong, terribly wrong, the way it occasionally does when people who don't trust each other are pulling off something illicit."

Another silence, as they both looked around the room. A room designed with thought: walls painted a quiet shade of blue-green, water colors that were abstract but not formidably so, furniture covered in noninstitutional chintz. A room to convey to putative parents the illusion of cozy domesticity.

"Linda, I won't kid you. People try to bribe us, of course they do. It's only a tiny percent of our clientele who do it, but the sums they offer are staggering. Well, let's say they stagger me. And the people go to work on anyone they think might be a pushover. Anyone they think can tip the balance. Me, the assistant director, the social workers, the secretaries, the trustees—couple of years ago, one of those pushy couples even made an overture to our receptionist."

"What could a receptionist do?"

Lee Hevessy shrugged. "She'd know names—it's conceivable. If she kept her ears and eyes open, she could tell them who was having a baby and they could approach the girl and dangle one of those staggering sums before her if she'd go a different route.... Listen, I'm not saying Rosie took them up on it, but like I said, it's conceivable."

"Rosie?"

"Rosalie Hinds. She was our receptionist. She's moved on since then. Moved up, I should say. Little Rosie. To think it was right at that desk outside that Claude Stanhope spotted her."

"Goodness. She was really your receptionist?"

"Ten to six, every day. The first face people saw when they came to New Beginnings. And what a face." Lee Hevessy's very different face allowed itself an appreciative grin. "She had this cute boyfriend used to call for her every evening. Nice-looking fellow. I'd see them go off hand in hand, I figured it was a sure thing. But I guess when someone like Stanhope comes along, even if he is thirty years older and not very good-looking—not in the least good-looking, if you know what I mean. But famous. And brilliant. All those studies about krill and plankton and the fragile web of life that's being damaged—do you understand that stuff?"

Linda didn't.

"Neither does Rosie, if you want my opinion. I doubt that Rosie even tries to understand. But he's

rich. Really rich. The Stanhope money—if you're a
pretty receptionist without a cent to your name, I
guess you don't sneeze at that. Even if you do have to
turn down a cute loverboy." Lee Hevessy's grimace
paid tribute to a Stanhope marriage settlement.

"We've had the same receptionist since then. Marcy
Lake. Very competent young woman, but she doesn't
look like Rosie. Oh, no, not like Rosie at all. I doubt
that some other member of our board will walk in and
be similarly smitten."

For a second, Linda was back at the dinner. That
cupcake face above the sugary shoulders, the high-
pitched, slightly blurred voice, the dazzled audience.
And of course her own resentment, her burning feeling of the inequity of fate. "Mrs. Stanhope spoke last
night at our annual dinner. Instead of her husband."

"I guess I did read it. He's on your board too, isn't
he, that generous man. Well, Rosie feathered her nest
all right, here at New Beginnings. But that's not the
kind of feathering you're looking for, is it?"

"Not exactly."

A sigh from that warm voice. "Linda, I wish I could
help you. Like I said, I have no doubt some money is
passed under the table. One way or other in this game,
it has to be. But I'm not on the receiving end, and
neither is anyone else in the agency that I know of. We
just bumble along, all of us. Doing a hard job and
getting no special reward for it."

Lee Hevessy went to the door and looked out, but
no one was waiting. "You would not believe how hard

this job is. Something no one considers. We hate turning people down. Sure we exclude some categories, we have to. If a couple is above a certain age, or if they have different religions or aren't strictly heterosexual, if someone isn't even a couple—forget it. But how else can we manage? A rare commodity and too many avid customers—what other way can we be fair? They hate us, sure they do, the people we turn down. The ones who are frantic for children and think it's our fault they can't get them.

"They're not the only ones who hate us." The voice could also, it seemed, turn sardonic. "There are experts who think we shouldn't be disposing of babies at all. There should be no adoptions. None. No babies taken from young mothers to satisfy rich would-be parents. Are the young mothers unwilling to bring up a child? Are they unable to? Do they have no money, no husband, no resources, maybe no place to live? Cross all that out. It doesn't signify. If they signed away their child, they did it under duress. We made them do it. We, the agency. There's a sacred bond of motherhood, and every day we violate it. Linda, you look surprised. You don't think people, intelligent people, really think this? See this book—the author lives right in this County. She'd tell you why you lost your baby. Because you shouldn't have gotten it in the first place. You pressured an ignorant girl when she was at her most vulnerable. No, my dear, of course I realize it isn't true. I'm just letting you in on the kind of thing we're up against. The ill-spirited and be-nighted attitudes we have to contend with.''

Something else Fran should have told her, she thought, as the monologue finally ended. People talk about themselves. They feel for you, they're sorry for you, they sincerely would like to help you. But it's their own concerns that call out their deepest emotions and most intense responses.

Well, next time she didn't plan to be so straightforward. For the coming interview, she was going to be devious. A neat approach, she had told Fran. One that could conceivably trap him if he really was involved.

He was also willing to see her. "Sure, come on over. I was going out to lunch, but I'll wait here," Jay Earling said when she called. He had an office on the second floor of a four-story building in downtown Plains. To get to the door that said *Jay Earling, Attorney at Law*, you walked past a dance studio, a hairdressing salon, a pottery group, and a dressmaker. You also, beyond the door, went past a secretary who, when Linda came, was knitting the sleeve of a blue sweater. He said right away he was glad to see her.

"Linda, what a tragedy. I wanted to call you this morning. That poor baby killed. I felt—no, responsible isn't the word. But in a way I suppose I was responsible," he said with a slow shake of the boyish head. "I acted for Marylou. I was the messenger, the delegate, the unwitting instrument of your calamity."

He had motioned her to a chair, but as if to remove any aspect of formality from their talk, he perched on the edge of his desk. "But somehow I couldn't frame the words. Even though half a dozen times I started to dial your number. Anything I could say—it seemed so inadequate. I know you'd given the baby up, she was no longer yours, but still, what a horror to hear she was dead."

Till now, every time she thought of Elena, it had been in her rosy beauty. She would picture the expansive smile, the convulsive joyfulness of arms and legs, she heard the delighted chortle. But as she gazed around Jay Earling's office, her mind's eye suddenly gave her a face fished up from that sluggish pond. Discolored skin, shriveled cheeks, mud clinging to the sparse eyebrows.

"A tragedy all around," Jay said, and brushed back the springy hair from his forehead. "That Marylou. I know you were furious at her, you had every right to be furious. What she tried to do was unpardonable. But still she was a decent girl. She had ambitions. Once over her muddled adolescence, she would have made something of herself."

"I believe it," Linda said. She added that he was nice to see her in the middle of a busy day.

"Not so busy." He picked up a pad, which presumably held his appointments. "What does this single practitioner have for the afternoon? Let's see. At two, I draw up for a client a divorce agreement that her ex probably won't be able to pay. At three, I inform a man who promises not to drink again he can get back his driving license. At four, I talk to someone who wishes he had the money to sue his neighbor. Nothing"—his hand performed a deprecatory wave—"to shake the world."

Nothing to hurt it either; the words hung in the air, but she didn't speak them. Instead, she looked around the office. Cases like that—they would not pay for a new paint job on walls where the old paint was flaking off, they wouldn't buy a rug to replace the threadbare one under her feet, they would not furnish a new venetian blind instead of this one with broken slats. They also did not keep his secretary from devoting her time to a knitted sweater.

His eyes took in her appraising glance. "Linda, when you called, you said you had something to ask me."

"Oh. Yes." Her hands clutched the arm rests of her chair. "I didn't realize how hard it was going to be."

"Take your time," he said.

"I mean, I have to contradict something I told you before."

"You know what they say about a foolish consistency." He gave her his eager smile. "The hobgoblin of small minds."

Little minds: she didn't correct him. She leaned forward. "Remember when you came to get the baby. God! Is it just two days ago?"

"Forty-eight hours," he assured her gently.

"Well, you suggested that some day maybe I'd want to adopt another. And in my distraught state, I turned it down flat. I said never, never. I said it was out of the question. I said—oh, I don't remember all the wild and categorical statements I made."

"Linda, when a woman is giving up her child, she's in no shape to say anything."

"Anyhow, I've been thinking it over. The thing is . . . I'm longing to try again."

In the silence, she heard cars outside on the street: the irate honks that meant two drivers were trying to maneuver into the same parking space.

"I'm not sure why you came to me," Jay said.

"It was just a hunch. You seemed so savvy when you handled that first adoption. I thought, a lawyer who has a local practice and knows so much about the subject."

"I do know something about the subject," he said, and got down from his perch on the desk. "The way someone in your position also must."

She spoke slowly. "I know, of course, that of the hundreds of unwanted babies born around here every month, some the reluctant mother or a member of her family keeps, some go to a person she happens to decide is suitable, some are disposed of through the accredited agencies. And also"—her gaze was still on that blemished wall—"some go to persons who because of one limitation or another aren't considered qualified by the agencies and have to resort to—to other tactics to get what they want."

"You found a child once on your own. I realize you're one of those the limitations apply to, but, Linda, you did find a child."

"That was a rare stroke of luck. I could wait ten years for something like it to happen again."

He pushed the appointment pad to one side. "There's something else. I'm talking off the top of my head, but I've always heard that to get a child by those other tactics, as you call them, you have to be rich. You have to be able to throw around the kind of money only people who live in a place like Mayhew Gardens can afford."

She kept her voice steady. "I'm surely not as rich as the people in Mayhew Gardens, but I don't spend my money on the things they do. I've been working a good many years, I've built up a nice little nest egg."

Across the desk, she could hear his sharp intake of breath. She sat looking down at her lap. God knows, with this office, this chintzy practice, he could use the money. If he says yes, that I've come to the right place, it means he's in it up to his neck. If he even speaks hypothetically, telling me how I might go about it, offering to look into details for me, it's a sign. He's playing it safe, but he's in it.

"Linda, you won't like what I'm going to say. It sounds cruel. It sentences you to what may be a lifetime without a child. But do you really want my advice? If there are those other tactics, steer clear of them. Don't get mixed up in that kind of shady operation. Why do I say anything so unyielding? For your own sake. To save you untold misery. Should I be specific? Well, when Marylou challenged the adoption, you did have a certain recourse. For your own reasons, you chose not to utilize it, but you could have. The courts were available for you to make your case. You could have argued that there was no duress. You could have cited all the counseling Marylou received from Fran and others before she made up her mind. You could have pointed to your own very superior qualifications for motherhood. You could have done all that''—he pushed back the springy hair from his forehead; the ingratiating gaze met hers—''You could have put up that good fight, and it's possible a judge would have ruled in your favor. 'Custody to Linda Stewart,''' his voice rolled out, in startling imitation of the ponderous one in court. ''None of that is an option in, shall we say, another kind of adoption. If the birth mother for any reason changes her mind, the adoptive mother has no alternative, none whatever, but to turn the baby over. A court that doesn't find the procedure legal in the first place won't offer its services in adjudicating it.''

His face still wore its boyish shine, but his exegesis, she had to admit, had been clear and forceful. He was sorry, he said finally, to have sounded so harsh. But you had to say what you believed, and without having any real experience in the matter, this was his belief.

She stood up. He'd been helpful, she said. She was grateful. That finished it; she was silent as he walked out with her, past the secretary who had added an inch to her sweater, past a woman who was unlocking the door of the pottery group and the thumps from a pi-

ano that emerged from the dance studio. But after he
left her, at the head of the stairs, she thought about it.
Helpful? Far from it. He'd have been helpful if he'd
said yes, he could arrange an illegal adoption for her.
That was what in her heart she had counted on. She
would set a trap, someone would fall into it, the whole
thing would be over. Now as she walked along the
street, she realized it was not going to be over as fast
as all that.

SIX

SHE DIDN'T CALL Marylou's father in advance. Two days after a daughter's death—she assumed he would be there, and he was. He was there and he was alone—that was the first thing that struck her. His solitariness. A man who had encountered tragedy—encountered it in the most public way possible—and no family members buzzing around, no neighbors knocking shyly with casseroles and sympathy, no friends assuring him that at this bleak time they would cover for him. After a few minutes with him, she understood. It was not just that in this house at the end of a street, neighbors might be sparse, or that a man working by himself in fact has no colleagues. But something about his hooded gaze, his arms folded defensively across his chest, his slightly averted head, made clear that he would always be solitary. It was his chosen mode. You knew men like that. Put them in the middle of a party, a picnic, a gathering, and they would be off to one side, munching their private sandwich, churning their private thoughts, not quite meeting anyone else's gaze.

Oh, he was perfectly civil. When he heard who she was, he asked her to come in, he invited her to sit down. But it was a parched kind of civility. It conceded nothing about his own needs. It opened itself to no generosity or consolatory words. It made no reference to the fact that he was a man bereft.

She sat in the chair he had indicated. A beautiful chair, its dark wood smooth and curved. A chair he had very likely made himself, Linda thought, seeing the flicker of pride as she rubbed her hands along the gleaming arm rests. But it wouldn't be beautiful to a young girl. Nothing in this room would. A seventeen-year-old girl would want cushions, throws, brightly colored rugs, the flutter of curtains. She wouldn't care if the furniture consisted of wooden crates so long as there was some jaunty material to cover them. The only material here was a dark green corduroy on the couch. A living room for a young girl to escape from.

Well, she escaped all right. Mr. Rogin said that right away. "You want to know what she was like at home? I couldn't control her, that's the truth. I tried everything; you better believe it. No use. Not with Marylou. A month shy of her fifteenth birthday and the boys were out there. Honking in front of the house. Like she was a dog in heat. How did they know? Word gets around. Those boys, they knew they wouldn't honk for nothing." He went over to the sideboard—something else he had made? "What did I try? You name it. I cut out her allowance. I stopped cooking dinner. Once I hit her. And I talked. I talked myself silly."

He stood with arms folded; the chunky body seemed to be all Marylou had inherited from him.

That and the dark coloring. And, of course, the stubbornness. "Then it changed. Instead of a different car every night, there was only one car. Only one boy, doing the shenanigans. A boy from Mayhew Gardens. You know what I mean." He gestured with sly contempt. "I knew the family. I once worked on their banister. I know all those families. I ought to. I fix their furniture often enough. They have one of their parties, and someone tilts too far back in an antique chair, and they come running to me. I'm supposed to fix it so it looks like new."

Again that flicker of gratification; doubtless he did fix it so it looked like new.

"That boy, I forget his name. Jerry... George..."

"Gil," she put in. It occurred to her that he was unaware of her special interest in all this. She had given her name and said she came from the Center, but grief or shame or just plain anger kept him from making connections; standing here, it didn't enter his mind that the product of Marylou's and Gil's shenanigans had been adopted by Linda Stewart.

"So that Gil, what was he doing here? Ha! We all know what he was doing here. I tried to tell her. The girls in his own neighborhood won't do it for him. They have too much sense, I told her. Too much self-respect. That's why he's after you. He'll use you and drop you, his parents will make him drop you even if he doesn't want to." He walked back and forth across the bare floor. "It was the God's honest truth. Those parents—I told you, I was in their house, I saw the pictures of him around. Gil at graduation. Gil winning the horseback-riding cup. Gil voted this and that. Their precious Gil, they used to say that some day he was going to be president. But did she listen? Not Marylou. Sixteen years old, and she was out there with him night after night.'' He stopped pacing, he took his bellicose stance in front of the window. ''Why do I tell you? You people, you think it's all fine.''

''Mr. Rogin, I don't understand.''

''You at the Center—you encourage it. You goad them on. Sixteen years old, why shouldn't they lie with their legs wide open for any boy that asks.'' He didn't look up, the square shoulders were turned away, but the note of disgust edged his voice.

''You have it all wrong. Encourage! That's the last thing—''

''You give them those pills. Or worse. They come in and tell you about it and you give them stuff. But do you ever say it's wrong? Do you let them know they're tramps? Do you send them home to their parents? That's what I would like to know. Do you tell them their parents know best?''

She pulled herself together. As she rattled off the usual arguments—more than a million teenagers becoming pregnant every year, thirty-one thousand of these younger than fifteen, the value of education in encouraging abstinence, the need for self-understanding—as she laboriously went through it, she thought, Do all parents feel like this at heart? Disgust at the whole idea of that raging sexuality.

Misunderstanding of those who seemingly abet it. Vengefulness at adults whose ideas deviate from their own. And of course, envy toward anyone who has influence with their children in areas where their own intervention has been summarily dismissed. Do even those sanctimonious donors at that head table cherish these misgivings? Even if they know they have to support the Center, do they also harbor ideas of nastiness and disgust?

No. Nothing like it. It's just this man who lives by himself, works by himself. This implacable loner. No one to mediate between him and a threatening world. His customers congratulate themselves on having found him. They don't make them like that any more, they say. The last of an old-fashioned breed, they exultantly say. But old-fashioned in other ways too, while he's fixing those antique chairs so they look like new, his mind shuttered against the menace of new ideas.

"Mr. Rogin, believe me, we don't encourage them to be sexually active. What we want is for them to gain some insight into their own behavior. What basic strength do they lack? How is school letting them down? Why does a girl of fifteen feel she has to have intercourse with her boyfriend?"

Another mistake. She saw the shudder start with the jolt of that square head, continue down through his whole body. "Lay with your legs open"—that's all right to say. "Like a dog in heat" about one's own daughter—that's all right. But "intercourse." Even

"sexually active"—she has overstepped. Gotten down
to the impermissible technicalities. Dirty words, nasty
expressions. Filth.

All right, start over. She said she really wanted to
talk about yesterday. About the time when the baby
had been allegedly brought to Marylou. Had he heard
anything, any hint at all, about Marylou's plans?

He excused himself and went into the kitchen—for
a minute she thought he might offer her some of the
coffee whose aroma she could detect. But when he
came back, he was empty-handed. "Parents are the
last to hear, didn't you know," he said; sarcasm had
taken the place of outrage. "Why would she think it
was necessary to tell me anything about that baby? She
didn't even tell me she was going to have it. We were
in the kitchen one day having breakfast, and she had
on her pajamas, and that's when I found out. Something in the oven, we used to say. So she's leaning over
to put some rolls into the stove, and all of a sudden it
hit me. 'Marylou, what goes on,' I said." He took his
former pose, arms folded across the outraged chest.
"You want to know something? She wasn't even
ashamed. She didn't make excuses. She just admitted
it right away. 'So what if I'm having a baby,' she said.
Miss Freshmouth. Like she might say, So what if I
have a cold."

"Did she say anything about the father?"

"She knew who it was, of course. That Gil. Like I
told her would happen, he had ditched her a couple of
months before. But for a year it was him. Gil, Gil, Gil.

All that money, but what good does it do us. He goes around scot-free, and she's walking around with her big belly."

He unfolded his arms and leaned against the veneered top of the sideboard. "It was bad enough when she went out like that. To school, to the movies, I don't know where all. Shopping. But when she expected me to go with her. I remember once, it was Memorial Day, there was the usual parade. They always have it, this big show along Harrison Boulevard. I guess none of her friends would put up with her, so she asks me will I go with her. That's how shameless she was. Her ninth month. This town where I have a reputation, I'm supposed to be seen with her at the Memorial Day parade."

Linda stood up; she walked over to the window. The uncurtained window. Maybe Marylou had stood here, looking out at the small front yard. A young girl barred from the parade because her father would not appear with her. What a pair they must have been. She needing comfort from him, he expecting contrition from her. And because of the kind of people they were, both of them suffering. Yes. He too, Linda thought. You could not in all fairness write off his suffering.

She sat again and by her tone tried to make clear that she was going to ask straight questions, and as if he too had had enough of passing exculpatory judgment on a dead daughter, he furnished simple answers. Did he know that Marylou had said she was going to take back the child? No. Had she made any preparations for doing this that he knew of? No. Did he find baby clothes or other equipment in her room after she died? Not that either. Would he have helped her if she'd brought a baby home? Certainly not, but that would not have stopped her.

Negative responses, unhelpful ones, but he sounded more subdued; the square face wore a regretful frown. It was how he might look explaining to some customer that she couldn't have the chair next Tuesday, to do the job right he would need ten days. "I always tried to do the best with her," he said. "From the time she was two years old."

"Two years?"

"I married her mother when Marylou was two."

"So you're her stepfather."

"Look here. I adopted that girl. I took care of her. I brought her up. Let me tell you something. She used to have this beautiful hair. Long, dark brown, below her shoulders. I like hair like that. It's the way a girl should look. Sometimes after her mother died, I used to brush it for her. It would get knotted up during the night, and she'd ask me to brush it." He looked down at his hands. Craftsman's hands, able to deal competently with long hair as well as antique wood. "So one day she comes home, it's all cut off. Like a mop. Oh, you saw it? So did she ask me if she could cut it? Did she consult me in advance?"

The stricken eyes glared. Cutting off her hair—it was part of the same intransigence as having that baby.

Linda looked at this father for a minute. This insulted father who had squirmed for nine months while Marylou carried that baby. Or rather, to his offended mind, there had not been a baby but simply an unseemly belly, a mortification, an affront to his position in the community. And then a baby did materialize. When he thought he had put the whole nasty business behind him, she brought it home. A five-month-old testament to laxness, to immorality, to defiance. His stepdaughter that he brought up did that to him. Another insult.

The thought of all this weighed on her, wearied her; she decided she'd heard all she could bear about Marylou's infractions, she might as well leave. But he suddenly surprised her. Marylou had their address, he said.

"Whose address?"

"Gil's parents. One twelve Drapers Pond Road. Not their name. Hildebrand. Not that. Just their address. I know that address."

"Where'd she have it?"

He shrugged. It was on a piece of paper. He found it on her dresser when he was going through her things. And don't ask him to tell more. How can anyone know what was going on in Marylou's head?

"Did she ever see them, that you know of? Get in touch with them? Mr. Rogin, did you hear her call them? No? You're sure? Well"—she was panting, possessed by urgency again—"was there anyone else she talked to? I mean, beside her school friends?"

He stood impassive. Just that woman.

"What woman?"

"From your office. What is it? That Center. Center for something." Even now that he had evidently decided to be forthcoming, he couldn't keep the contempt out of his voice. "You know who I mean. Tall woman, red hair, always wears those mannish suits. What's her name? Starts with an M. Max something."

"Maxine?"

That was it.

"Maxine Hammond came here to talk to Marylou? You're sure of that?"

Now he was the one to signal impatience. He looked at his watch. Not the surreptitious glance of one trying to be polite. A pointed observation, meant to convey to a visitor that time was running out.

"Mr. Rogin, it just might be important. Please try to remember. Did you ever hear what they were talking about? Even a word, a hint? Because if Marylou had been having problems, the kind of problems we handle, the normal thing would've been for her to come to the Center. So for one of our counselors to meet her here at home..."

He doesn't know. He can't help. The whole thing beats him. When Marylou talked to anyone, she made sure the door to her room was closed. And she didn't explain. He heard her say "Goodbye, Maxine," and then she told him the woman worked at the Center, but no explaining. Why should she explain to him? He was only her father. Since when do fathers rate explanations.

He didn't try to hide the rancor. He held the door open for her, a man who might feel grief for his daughter's death, but right now was grieving more for the hurts inflicted during her life.

SEVEN

SHE STOPPED AT the nearest phone booth to call the
Center, but Maxine wasn't there. Maxine had left
early. Personal business. Linda slowly hung up the
receiver. Maxine was a colleague. A relatively new
one—she'd come to work at the Center just six months
ago—but still a colleague. A talk with Maxine would
take place in her own office, at her own desk, while she
put some questions and Maxine either came up with
the answers or proved evasive in a way that might
constitute an answer in itself.

The alternative—going to see Gil's parents—would
be very different.

She walked out of the phone booth. Was it just this
morning that she had invented herself in the role of
detective? In the space of six hours, she had pushed
herself into it, served her apprenticeship, proved herself. But she didn't like it. Fran said she would not like
it, and Fran was right. She got back in her car, but she
drove slowly to the area called, with edgy respect,
Mayhew Gardens, and when she got to Drapers Pond
Road, she slowed further—that was how she saw the
sign next to a gatepost that said Stanhope. She put on
her brakes. Maybe she would get a glimpse of the
mansion into which a pretty little receptionist, to the

amazement of everyone, had been summarily catapulted.

Not a chance. Nothing was visible. Not a turret, not a window, not a slope of roof. Only a driveway winding between two rows of beech trees, and at one of the gate posts, a small crowd of people.

When Linda got out of her car, the crowd resolved itself into five people. One who looked like a gardener—yes, there was his truck across the street—two women who had been going by on bicycles, and a postman, all listening with varying degrees of sympathy to an irate young man who held a camera like a prop before him. "I'll tell my editor," he was saying. "My editor knows how to deal with people like that."

Linda joined the circle. An extra person in his audience: it roused the young man to new heights of outrage. "She didn't have to do it. It was pure meanness. All she had to do was ask me to stop."

Stop what? Linda put out her hands in an interrogatory gesture, and the young man responded to it. Though he had plainly told his story to the others, he repeated it to Linda. He'd just wanted to get a picture for the Riverview Times. They were running a column on Dr. Stanhope, who was returning tomorrow night, returning after all those months in that frigid place, and the editor thought a picture might be nice. So he went in and snapped the wife. Was that so bad? Did it call for such a wild reaction? If you were married to a famous man, you ought to be used to that kind of publicity. And a photographer can't stand around saying, Please may I. He'd never get anyplace if he did that. So he just took her picture. The woman standing on the terrace with her baby. And she tricked him. When she saw him and walked toward him, she didn't even look angry. She was smiling. As though she'd say, Oh, let me comb my hair. Or maybe, Wait till I take off the sweater. Even though she looked perfectly nice. Better than nice. This short checked skirt and the green top with swooping sleeves. So he stood there, holding the camera, and what does she do but grab it and smash it with a rock. Then she takes out the film and smashes that too.

"She cursed at me. She said, 'How dare you take my picture without asking me first.' Then the curse words. A woman like that cursing—I was really shocked."

He wasn't shocked, Linda saw. He was wounded. Deeply hurt. Also, he was even younger than she'd thought at first—the pitted skin and tremulous mouth of an eighteen- or nineteen-year-old. Probably he wasn't a regular staff member and there was no editor to go to bat for him. Maybe he'd applied for a job, and some editor had said, Let's see how enterprising you are, kid. Let's see what you can get. And what had he gotten but a curse. A curse and a broken camera.

"If she'd just said a word. But no. The little rich bitch had to ruin it, a brand new camera. Practically brand new. See what she did?" His beseeching glance accosted each of them in turn. "You're my witnesses."

Well. Not exactly. None of them answered. None of
them offered help. The gardener, in fact, was backing
off already—he crossed the street and got into his
truck. A second later, the postman followed. As for
the women, they shook their heads in commiseration,
as Linda did, and offered mollifying words, but that
was it. The whole extent of their cooperation. The
young man realized after a while. No one would in-
terfere. No one was going past these imposing stone
gates to tell a woman she should have acted better to
an aspiring young photographer. Nor would anyone
else come along. He looked dolefully up and down the
road, but this was not the kind of neighborhood where
people strolled past. "Nasty story, isn't it?" one of the
women said to Linda, after the young man, facing the
facts, had hugged his broken camera to his breast and
drove off. Linda nodded. Very nasty. Nasty and also
puzzling. When you thought of the dress Rosalie
Stanhope had worn to the Center dinner, a dress that
both by its color and its cut had said, Look at me, look
at me, you had to find it somewhat puzzling that she
would not want her picture taken.

However, Rosalie Stanhope was not her problem.
The Hildebrands were, and five minutes later she
pulled up in front of their house.

It was the kind of house Lee Hevessy might have
had in mind when her caustic voice referred to "this
classy suburb." Red brick, with dazzling white col-
umns to hold up a front portico, a long veranda running the length of the house, tile roof. Inside, more

splendors. Mrs. Hildebrand herself answered the door, and when Linda gave her name and said she worked for the Center for Teen-Age Counseling and Reproductive Health, she was told to come in dear, come right in. You didn't come right in. You went through an imposing hall, and then a living room where even a quick glance spotted the gleam of antique rugs and furniture, and finally you got to the sun parlor, where you were meant to feel comfortable instead of awed. Wicker furniture, a profusion of hanging plants, windows looking out on an admirable view, and—trust Mr. Rogin—on a small table, a picture of Gil. She concluded it must be Gil. Someone fresh-faced and dark-haired, snapped as he stood next to a bicycle.

Mrs. Hildebrand followed her glance. "Our son. Beautiful, isn't he?"

"Yes."

"Good too. Perfect, just about."

"I'm sure."

Mrs. Hildebrand sighed in contentment: a small woman full of nervous little gestures. Her hand went out to move the photograph a fraction of an inch. Then she said not all parents were as lucky as they were—didn't she know it. That's why the Center was so important. She'd been meaning to contribute but she just never got around to it. She knew the wonderful work.

Linda interrupted at this point. She explained that her visit was for a very different reason. Had Mrs. Hildebrand read the local paper of two days ago?

Then did she read about the girl who'd been found drowned along with her child? She was here in connection with that story. That terrible story. In fact—her throat thickened—she was the adoptive mother of that drowned child.

"You adopted the baby? When it was born?" Mrs. Hildebrand tugged at the sleeve of her sweater.

"Yes."

"Then how come—"

"Marylou came three days ago and said she wanted it back. I didn't want to fight her. In my position as a teenage counselor, I didn't see how I could."

"Oh, my. Oh, my." The woman got up and moved an ashtray. Then she moved it back. She pulled a dead leaf off an ivy plant. She twitched the picture of Gil forward another inch. Oh, my, she kept saying in her thin voice.

Oh, my, because of the nature of what she'd just heard? Or because of an awareness of her special relation to it? Linda didn't find out because there was a noise from inside. The woman listened—then with a look of vast relief, she turned. "My husband. He's home early. Excuse me—be right back."

She was not right back. Linda got up and studied the lawn, she examined the plants, she found another picture—Gil in cap and gown—and looked at that. She was opening an album—Gil as a child—she found on a wicker table when they finally came in.

"This is Linda Stewart. My husband, Dwight Hildebrand."

He gave a bow of mock courtesy. He was a tall man—tall, sunburned, handsome. In his gray business suit, his striped tie, his white shirt, he could be any of the hundreds of commuters who stepped on the city-bound train every morning, and looking a little fatigued, a little the worse for wear, got off it in late afternoon.

If Mr. Hildebrand was fatigued, he didn't show it. "Who might Linda Stewart be?" he said with the same ironic civility.

Well. In all that time, his wife had surely told him. But evidently he thought it conferred an advantage to make Linda repeat the story, and in her pedantic voice she went through it again. Local paper. Mother and baby. Hommocks Pond. Drowned.

Mr. Hildebrand waved a negligent hand. "This beautiful suburb, but we're not exempt, it seems, from sordid incidents like that. We can't escape."

She looked at him: the dignified disapprobation, the purposeful unconcern. "Oh, for God's sake. This is crazy. It's not just any child we're talking about. It was mine. A child that for five months I brought up. And also"—she looked for a moment at Gil's guileless eyes in the silver frame—"a child that Marylou had with your son."

In leisurely fashion, a man who had no reason to be rushed, Mr. Hildebrand sat down. "It's a little presumptuous of you to say so." The hard words did not detract from the air of derisive politeness.

"Marylou had no doubt about it. All the time she was pregnant."

"What makes you think you can believe everything this Marylou said?"

"She had no reason to lie."

"If she's the kind of girl you say, I can think of plenty of reasons."

"I didn't say. You did. Actually, she was a gutsy, ambitious girl. She had planned an interesting life. She wanted to go to designer school."

For a second it seemed as if Mrs. Hildebrand would speak. She opened her mouth, made a couple of throat-clearing sounds. But her husband's careless voice got there first. "This is a ridiculous conversation. I'm puzzled about what you're doing here, Miss Stewart. What is it you want?"

"I want to issue a reward to help find out who murdered them." Her breath went out; all the way here, she had practiced saying it. "I can't afford it myself."

"Why come to us?"

Round and round: combative assertion and casual denial, chasing each other's tail in this hospitable sunroom. "I told you. Your—" No. Don't say "grandchild." Grandchild is a sacred word. It connotes love, tenderness, pride, joy. "Your son's child."

"I believe I told you that we don't accept that."

"I could find plenty of people, friends of both Marylou and your son, to support my contention."

Her voice was steady, but she wondered if this was true.

"You know, Miss Stewart," he said. "It all strikes me as curious. You come here with a scurrilous story, and then you actually expect us to give you money."

When she was considering the adoption, a standard check had been done on Gil. His health, his mental stability, his rank in school. But some information about the father had also inevitably crept in. Chief executive officer of one corporation, on the board of two others, architect of the buyout of still another—the facts were available to anyone who cared to look for them. Ruthless, her informant had told her. One of those ruthless businessmen. But don't let it bother you, Linda, the genes are okay.

She repeated that the money would not be for her, it was for a reward.

"To me it sounds preposterous. An unworkable and preposterous idea." He went over to the door. "I think we might end this conversation, Miss Stewart."

"No, Dwight, wait. Let's hear what she has to say." Flustered, nervous, thin-voiced—but Mrs. Hildebrand was not to be counted out of it. Linda saw her lay a finger on her husband's arm.

"I want to know who did it. Who would drown a young woman and a baby? The police think Marylou was part of a drug gang in the high school, somehow it led to murder. I think it's more likely that it had to do with selling babies. Someone offered Marylou a good price for her child, and that's why she took it back. Whatever it was, I want to find out.''

"What good will it do?" the thin voice asked.

"The same good it does any parent who goes to court after a beloved child has been killed. I used to wonder about them, those couples who sit there day after day. Now I understand. They feel vindictive—it's better than grieving, it dulls the pain. They want heads to roll. They want to make sure there's some compensatory suffering.''

"How about the police? Are they in favor of this reward?''

All at once, it took on reality. Reward: it translates into specific sums, it offers enticements, its terms appear on posters to be hung on trees and lampposts. "I haven't told the police. I don't know what they'd say. Yes, maybe I do know. They think I shouldn't get involved.''

"Did it ever occur to you the police might be right?'' the man asked.

This time she turned frankly toward one of the pictures. She remembered Mr. Rogin: their precious son, that they figure will some day be president. "Maybe your son wouldn't agree.''

"Leave him out of this," the man said, and suddenly the ironic courtliness was gone. Under the tan, his face reddened, a vein throbbed in his neck. "I warn you.''

A warning? What kind of warning? "I just mean, he might be in favor of offering a reward. I could ask

him. Where is he? What college?" And when neither
of them answered, "Oh, come on. It would be easy
enough to find out. It's in the high school records,
what college they all go to. I won't do it," she added
as she saw the man clench his fist. "I don't intend to.
I just wonder if they were ever in contact. Marylou
and your son, after the baby was born."

"Of course not. Why should they be?"

She took a deep breath. She laid her hand on the
small wicker table where Gil looked out in cap and
gown. "Well, then, did *you* ever hear from her? Has
she ever contacted you?"

"Us!" Mr. Hildebrand took a step toward her, and
a wild idea about the drastic action these two protective parents might be capable of crossed her mind.
Maybe this is what it means to play at being a detective. Not the pushy overtures, not the unseemly intru-
sions into other people's lives, not the supply of
questions worked up in advance, but simply the wild
idea that flits for an instant across the susceptible
mind.

"Why in the world would that girl contact us?"

"She had your address written down."

"Who told you that?"

"Her father."

Mr. Hildebrand thought this over; he was again in
control. "That father. Why don't you ask him for the
money?"

With his casual, his insolent tone, he managed to
make it sound like a jest, but she answered seriously.

"He would never agree. He's a stubborn, bitter man. The kind who keeps his distance from the world at the same time as he slavishly craves its good opinion. Just the worst kind to bring up a feisty, independent girl. He stifled her. He held her back. He made no allowance for any ideas she might have on her own. All those plans she had for her life, but she got no encouragement from him. So she did what lots of them do when home is closed off as a place of support. She looked to sex for commendation and warmth. And when she got pregnant, she disgusted him. That's all he felt—humiliation and disgust, and he let her know it."

Did she move them? Was there a tremor on that face that could look arrogant and indifferent at once? She'd spoken to shake them, but she was the shaken one. For the first time, she focused on the tragedy in terms of Marylou as well as the baby. An aspiring life snuffed out. A brave ambition stopped in its tracks.

"This reward," Mrs. Hildebrand said, and the restraining finger was again on her husband's arm. "How much were you thinking of?"

Ah. She shook her head. She hadn't settled on a figure. Ten thousand? Twenty thousand?

"Suppose we do decide to help," Mrs. Hildebrand said in the thin voice that after all could take over a conversation from her husband and guide it into a new course. "Where should we get in touch with you? The Center?"

"Yes. Well, no, better not." She told them her address and phone number before she walked with them to the door. Then she was in her car again, looking back at the house. When she trained people who were going to work with teenagers, she told them what to attend to. "Don't just listen to what the boy or girl is saying. Watch out for pauses, hesitations, nuances. Observe the facial expression. Learn to understand poses and postures. Body language." That woman's restraining finger on her husband's arm—was that body language? The vein beating in his throat when Linda suggested contacting his son—was that?

She drove fast, down the winding road that had more traffic now: men coming back from the station, cars going to pick up men at the station. Should she have prodded him further? Taken advantage of the momentary lapse in his control? She went over and over the conversation, thinking of things she had said, might have said. She would keep doing this. Not scrutinizing the actions of others, but assessing her own performance. Another thing Fran had neglected to mention. If you took on an unfamiliar role, you also took on a whole new set of uncertainties. Self-searching, introspection. It was what was in store for her tonight unless she did something about it.

She would do something, she thought as she drove into her parking lot. Call Harold. Dear decent considerate Harold. With his great tact, his sweet concern, he had probably decided he had best stay away for another couple of days, but she would tell him otherwise. He would bring an arrangement of fall flowers. He would compliment her dress. He would take her to the best restaurant. Solace, comfort, forgetfulness; she could use an evening of that. But as she went to the phone, it rang.

"Miss Stewart? This is Bettina Brody."

"You must have the wrong—"

"Oh, please don't hang up. Please. I really do need you." It was a hoarse, scratchy woman's voice, the voice of one pushing out the words with an effort. Linda sat down. A client of the Center? No, it sounded like someone more mature. A troubled parent, perhaps.

"Miss Stewart, I read about you in the newspaper. I'm so sorry. Such a terrible thing, and I—"

Her finger was just pressing down the receiver— there was just so much you could stand—when the next sentence jumped through the wire. "...don't want the same thing to happen to me."

"What are you talking about?"

EIGHT

OAK STREET WAS PLEASANT. Not an area like May-hew Gardens, but accessibly pleasant. The kind of street you fantasize about if you live on the fourth floor of an apartment complex. A street where groups of children wander with proprietary ease from the jungle gym in one yard to the swing in another, where the woman at number 42 calls out, Who wants cookies, where the one at 38 says, Bobby, didn't I hear your mother calling you for dinner ten minutes ago? Dinner time now. A taxi dislodged two men with briefcases, a voice called to Alice and Pam to get in here this instant.

Forty-six was also pleasant: white shingle with green shutters. There were blinds in the downstairs windows, and a white curtain blew out of a partly open window upstairs. She went up a front walk bordered with flowers that were long past their prime, she had rung the bell twice before she remembered: try the back.

More flowers along the side; marigolds and chrysanthemums now grown leggy, and a companionably low hedge that separated this lawn from the one next door. A small boy pulling a wagon looked over the hedge at her. "You our new baby-sitter?" he asked.

His judgmental stare continued even after she explained that she wasn't. "Letti can't come any more; my mom says a new girl is coming to baby-sit me tonight." She told him to have a nice time with the new baby-sitter, then she went around to the back.

Here she realized she hadn't fully appreciated Oak Street. In front, seeing the sidewalk, the mandatory rows of foundation planting, the flower beds, you assumed that was the whole story. Decorous suburbia. You had no idea that beyond the backyard there was a strip of woods that had been allowed to grow wild. It might be no more than twenty or so yards wide—impossible to tell in the growing dusk—but what a bonanza for children who could play hide and seek there, search for whatever treasures lay squirming under the layers of leaf and mold, pretend, as a tree cut off sight of their home, that they were gone for the week. Contrived adventure. Make-believe danger. She stopped for a minute beside a sprawling viburnum. When she used to bend over Elena at night, she would see not only the curled-up limbs, the damp hair, the delicious curve of cheek, but a young girl in the stages of growing up. Elena bringing home her new best friend from second grade. Elena trying out roller skates for the first time. Elena welcoming the gang to her pajama party. And those scenes were played out against the background of a house like this. An apartment playground adjacent to a parking lot would be fine for the first three or four years—after that, a child should be able to run at will to the house next

door, to ride up and down on her bike, to fling her toys
on the steps before coming with muddy feet into the
house.

Toys on the back steps now, she noted with surprise. A broken truck, a rag doll minus one arm. Odd.
From the fervor in that telephone voice, the desperation, she had taken for granted that the three-week-old
child Bettina Brody was afraid of losing was her only
one. But of course you could be fervent about a child
if there was another in the family or even two others.
After she got to the top landing and rang the bell, she
stooped to pick up the truck, and that was when she
heard it. The sound of a shot, and, simultaneously,
over the place where her head had been, a swoosh of
air, a blast. Her fingers closed hard around the truck.
It was a cheap tin one; a ragged fender cut into the
tender skin under her thumb; she felt the spot of blood
before she saw it. For an instant, that blood trickling
down her hand seemed the worst aspect of her predicament. Then she saw herself as she must look to an
observer. A woman crouched over a straw mat who
can't decide whether it's better to stay down or, with
a semblance of dignity, to regain a standing position.

Stay down. By all means, stay down. But she heard
voices, and it appeared that observers were in fact
coming around the side of the house. A woman in a
tan suit trimmed with black braid, a couple slightly
behind her. There was a railing around the top landing of the stairs, and she reached for it. Not so easy to

stand after all. And no dignity; her knees shook and her breath came in gasps as she pulled herself up.

The woman, however, could move quickly. Leaving her companions, she walked over to the steps. "I beg your pardon," she said in a tone of deep affront, as if Linda had insulted her.

Linda was on her feet but she still held onto the railing. "Did you hear a shot?"

"A shot? Oh, yes. The children around here play with BB guns. Their parents should never allow it. I believe it's against the law."

"I thought there was a real gun."

The woman didn't bother to answer this. She called to the couple who for some reason—was it the sight of Linda?—were hanging back. "A splendidly planted backyard," she told them. "Look at those lilacs—I wish it were lighter so you could really appreciate. And very spacious," she said. "This backyard by itself measures sixty-five by eighty-two, but that stretch of woods over there is eminent domain, and that makes the property seem even larger."

She pointed to the stand of trees, and Linda's gaze followed her finger. Contrived adventure—is that what she thought? Make-believe danger? With the light dimming quickly, the foliage seemed dark, even black; if anyone was in there—if anyone had been there—impossible to detect it.

The man and woman were still staring at her. Was her hand bleeding? She put it into a pocket and came all the way down the stairs. "A Mrs. Brody called me," she said. "Bettina Brody. About a baby."

"Brody?" The woman in the tan suit exhorted her charges to note this stretch of level lawn: perfect for croquet or badminton. Or a patio over there next to the bed of lilies. Or if one was interested in growing vegetables in a serious way.... They liked that idea? Here was their idea spot. She added in a perfunctory way that Linda must be mistaken.

"Isn't this number forty-six? Forty-six Oak?" And when the woman nodded—"She said come to the back door. If the front door didn't...I mean, if the bell..."

"Of course it wouldn't help to go to any door," the woman said crisply. "The house is vacant and I'm the only one with keys. Our office has an exclusive. If you would like my card?"

Linda looked at it. Summit Real Estate, it said. 229 Grand Street. And in the corner, Allison Lorrimore.

"I'm sorry, Miss Lorrimore. But this woman, Bettina Brody..."

"The Halsteads lived here until a month ago," Miss Lorrimore said, "but Dr. Halstead went on sabbatical, they're renting the house furnished for a year. If you're interested, you can call my office in the morning."

It was Linda's dismissal, her injunction to say no more about the foolishness of guns or babies or nonexistent Brodys. She was spoiling the ambience, interfering with a sale. Her perverse comments were out of place. Even her appearance was out of place. She had jumped to action when she got that phone call, not stopping to change the blouse she had worn all day or comb her hair. Now the dismay in the eyes of this couple interested in serious vegetable growing told her how she must look.

The small boy was no longer there when she went around to the front—had the new baby-sitter come?—and no shots sounded as she got into her car. But the shot sounded in her ears. That sharp and crackling retort: unmistakable. Someone tried to kill me, she would tell Lieutenant Wilkerson. They had this perfect trick to get me out there, they conned me into the back of this empty house—well, they thought it would be empty—and there was the ideal place for someone with a gun, only just as they had me in position, this real estate agent.... Oh, a woman's voice. A scratchy woman's voice. Mrs. Bettina Brody, but the Brodys don't live there.

Whom does she suspect? She suspects everyone; at the moment the world has for her the aspect of a grand design for treachery.

However, Lieutenant Wilkerson was not at his desk to hear this flaming diatribe. Sorry, gone for the night, does she want to speak to anyone else? Very well, Miss, we'll tell the Lieutenant you called.

NINE

SHE DID GET HIM on the phone the next morning, though by then her report was not so incisive. Someone tried to kill me. Or maybe not—each time she went over the scene, she changed her mind. It was the real thing; it was a harmless crank on the phone, and that shot, as the real estate agent said, was nothing but a BB gun.

However, as if there were no quiver in her voice, Wilkerson asked the pertinent questions. Mostly, he asked to whom she'd been talking during the day. She told him—Lee Hevessy, director of New Beginnings; Jay Earling; Marylou's father: Mr. and Mrs. Hildebrand—and waited for the inevitable burst of criticism. But all he said was, considering her theory about selling babies, he could understand her choice of the first three. But the Hildebrands? What in the world?

She was the one to pause now. Sitting over her empty cup of coffee, she said he must know they were the parents of the boy who had fathered Marylou's child. But considering the kind of people they were and the hopes they had for the son, the last thing they would want was for that knowledge to come out. So suppose Marylou had gone to them with the baby. Suppose she threatened to expose their son unless they gave her money. Suppose they then—her voice failed. She remembered that inviting sun room with the wicker furniture, the plants. She saw Mrs. Hildebrand moving an ashtray a quarter of an inch. She heard the venom in Mr. Hildebrand's voice as he said, I warn you.

Lieutenant Wilkerson cleared his throat. "Miss Stewart, I hope you're through asking questions. I hope you're going to your regular work this morning."

"Oh, I am. I am." Half true: she did plan to go to work. But through with questions? There was still the business of Maxine. What did Maxine have to do with Marylou? Why did she go to the girl's house? Questions she certainly intended to put as soon as she saw Maxine in the office.

And as it happened, she saw Maxine before getting to the office. She had been asked to stop this morning at the station. Louella was planning to take a leave from her nurse's job, and a new candidate was coming on the train; because Linda drove within two blocks of the Riverview station anyhow, would she do the picking up? The woman had described what she would be wearing and Linda described herself; a simple matter for them to spot each other; she saw the woman at the same instant as the woman, with a relieved smile, saw her. But looking down the platform, Linda saw something else. Maxine had also got off the train and promptly walked over to a green car that belonged—could it be?—to Jay Earling.

"You're Miss Stewart?" The new woman was at her car window.

"Do you mind? I just realized—well, look. There's the taxi office over there, they'll surely—yes. And tell Debbie to cancel my appointments. Tell her something came up."

There was a snag getting out of the parking lot, but she caught up with the green car on Maple. Definitely Jay; only one car was between them, she could see plainly the ingratiating profile, the hand going up to push back that boyish forelock. Once free of the station area, she found traffic was light. Nine ten: the children were already in school, the commuters on the train—she had no trouble following. No trouble even though she was new at this. Linda Stewart finding aptitudes in herself she has never guessed at: it turns out she can hang back, then accelerate, then if need be come to an abrupt stop; she can even lose them and catch them again in the tangle of traffic on Lincoln. Why Lincoln? Why are they heading into the heart of Riverview? Two people in a scheme together, a scheme that surely involves babies born to the Center clientele—where are they going?

They were going to the courthouse; it was the last place she expected. She took her foot off the accelerator when they turned in at the parking lot for that imperial building; only the honk of a car behind reminded her to keep driving. She drove around the block; she didn't enter the lot herself until she saw them—Maxine towering a good three inches over Jay—walk together to the recessed entrance.

Once inside, bewilderment. All the courtrooms and halls and offices toward which two people can head. She stood immobile till she saw that the door that said Part 2 was open. "You going in or out?" asked a woman behind her, a woman carrying a paper bag in one hand and pulling two children with the other. "In"—because in the third row she had spotted Maxine, or at least her gray hat. If you have to tail someone, make sure it's someone tall: adage for today. She took a seat in the next-to-last row, from where she could see them.

Or not exactly them. Maxine might be in the third row, but it wasn't till Linda leaned sideways that she spotted Jay Earling in row one. She took off her jacket. A courtroom usually holds for her an irresistible fascination. Even a courtroom for arraignments, as the man in the next seat informed her this one was. Once she had a client who killed her own infant. Well, not exactly killed. After the girl gave birth alone in her own room, she had simply walked out for two days, a gesture of frenzy and melancholy that presented her, on her return, with a small corpse, and when her trial came up, Linda sat through all of it. Not just the day when she herself was due to testify. All five heartrending and compelling days.

No fascination today. She resented even the proclamation of the clerk telling them all to rise for the judge, even the argument between two attorneys at the bench, even the shuffling parade of defendants walking in under escort and settling themselves on a bench—all these seemed to her a cruel delay, an indefensible postponement of the time when she would find out what that pair was up to. She could no longer see Jay, but Maxine still was visible. Maxine, whose shoulders in the man-tailored shirt were leaning forward tensely. Why the tension? Not, surely, for the first case, which was a young man arrested for—what? She turned to her knowledgeable friend on the left. "I can't hear. What are they saying?"

"Purse snatching. First offense. Hard to make it out at first but you get used to it. It's a knack," he said kindly. He was an elderly man, dressed in tweed suit and bow tie, and he added that he was a regular. He preferred a real trial, but he would make do with arraignments. TV and movies couldn't hold a candle.

"I see."

"This judge at least speaks up, that's more than some of them do. You can hear him, can't you?"

She heard. The purse snatcher, who had made the mistake of knocking down his victim as well as taking her purse, pleaded guilty, and the judge pronounced the sentence: three to six.

The next one would not get off so easy, her neighbor told her. "See that court officer standing behind him? That means they think he might try something." Right again. No plea bargaining this time. The defendant did not in fact try anything, he simply stood with head rigid and hands hanging while his attorney talked. She caught a few words: "dark," "garage," "gun," "very dark." And whatever the import of the attorney's plea, it was unavailing. The judge set a date for the trial and also twenty-five thousand dollars' bail, which the defendant was evidently unable to pay because an attendant led him out the door by which he had come.

"The judge doesn't like that. Doesn't like when they insist on a trial. Clutters up the courts." Her tour guide.

"I see."

"But he'll zip through the next one. He's partial to women, doesn't much care for putting them in jail. Watch and see."

She watched. She particularly watched because when the next one was called—her name was Jenna Walsh and she was about eighteen—Jay Earling rose and met her at the bench. The mother of the children was now opening bags of candy that crackled wildly; Linda heard "gloves," "store," "money," and then nothing. Not the response of the girl, surely not the words of Jay, whose slight figure moved expressively in front of the judge.

"I can't hear."

"Shoplifting," her friend said. "First offense. She'll get a suspended sentence, she's too pretty to put in jail."

The girl was not pretty; that was evident when she turned. Or, rather, she might have been pretty with the addition of twenty pounds and a different expression.

As it was, under her red hair she looked pinched, a face of sallow concavities. She wore no makeup, but still there was something artificial about her, as if a layer of experience or maybe suffering were stretched tightly over the features.

The tightness didn't change. Even when the judge said, "I'm going to let you off, but stay out of trouble," the set mouth didn't relent. You knew that expression. If you worked with teenagers, you saw it often enough. Disdain, detachment, indifference— whatever you called it, it served to obscure the fright. Oh, yes, they were frightened, these girls. Frightened that help might not be forthcoming, and also practiced at accepting it as their due. Once the judge had his say, the girl didn't acknowledge her lawyer. No cursory thanks. Not the simple concession of goodbye. Without a glance at him, or indeed at the woman peering from her third-row seat, she turned and stalked out, a figure in jeans and boy's cap and yellow jacket who couldn't be bothered thanking the pair whose machinations had gotten her sprung.

Well, why thank them? It was a business transaction. They would take care of her, pay her expenses, get her out of her scrapes, and eventually, for whatever price had been agreed on, she would turn over to them the child she was presumably carrying under the loose jacket. Yes. Linda had it figured out. Maxine to link up with the girls, and Jay, whom she had prematurely written off, to attend to the technicalities, and the two of them in possession, after a few months, of one of the most valuable commodities available for marketing these days.

"Going already?" Her friend in the bow tie.

"Yes."

"You ought to stay. This next case, the fellow—"

She was not to know what the fellow did. Up ahead, she saw people slouch to their feet so Maxine could slide past. This time Linda didn't hang back. She was not trying to be invisible, just the opposite. She got to the hall a second after Maxine did.

"Goodness, Linda, I didn't expect to see you here."

"I guess you didn't." Her tight-lipped rejoinder as she walked abreast of the boxy suit. "Are you in a rush? I thought we could have coffee."

"Well, I—" Maxine peered around the hall. It had gotten more crowded; the girl in the yellow jacket was not to be seen. "Why not?" she resignedly said. "There's a coffee shop two doors down."

TEN

"SO THE JIG'S UP," Maxine said.

"I suppose you might say so." She had thought the coffee shop would be an unsightly place, bearing the flavor of the noise and squalor of the courthouse, but in fact bright lights shone on the tiled walls, and blue and white checked tablecloths covered each small table.

"Something appalling like that, you always think you have the particular talent to keep it secret." Maxine laid her pocketbook on the table.

"I wouldn't know," Linda said coldly.

"I thought, if I just exercise caution—oh, coffee and danish," she told the waitress.

Just coffee for Linda.

"And then all the other subterfuges. Making a big deal, a whole elaborate story, about the other details of your life. I remember once sitting at lunch with you and Fran and talking about some new wallpaper for my kitchen. To tell the truth, I can live without wallpaper. But I thought, if that's what they associate me with, wallpaper in a pattern of blues and grays, if that's their image of me, maybe I can get by."

Linda looked up; the waitress put the danish in front of her, and she gave it a vicious shove across the table.

"And then these clothes. These boring man-tailored clothes. You wouldn't know it, but I love stuff that's daring and a little wild. Even vulgar. The other day I tried on this bright red dress with a peasanty neck. The same red as my hair. God, I was tempted. But then I thought, No, they can't think of me as even the least little bit slutty, I have to be the essence of respectable guidance counselor."

"You really thought clothes would help?" She looked at Maxine's somber gray jacket, which was hanging on the chair.

"If you're desperate, you'll try anything." The coffee was steaming, but Maxine took two long gulps. "Linda, must you tell the others?"

"The others?"

"Fran, Roy Gardiner, the directors."

"I hardly think—"

"I really need this job. Right now you probably can't believe anything I say, but it's true." She cut the danish into four pieces, but she didn't eat it. "I'm not so employable. Thirty-nine—people don't want to start with you. Besides, I particularly wanted to be here. This County."

"I can understand that." Linda's fingers drummed on the table.

"You think it's a sign of weakness, don't you?"

"Well . . ."

"I wanted to be near her. Okay, spy on her, if you insist. Get a glimpse of her once in a while. Linda, I know you think it's crazy after what you just saw, but I keep having these delusive hopes. She's going to turn a corner. She'll suddenly straighten out. If it's your own daughter, you can't help it. You keep seeing the worthwhile person under those ravaged looks."

"Maxine, what?...Daughter?..."

"I know. It's the names you heard in court. Jenna Walsh. It's partly my fault. I did tell the truth on my application. One daughter. Joyce. But what I didn't say, when she was eleven, she changed her name to Jenna. And then of course the last name is different because I took back my maiden name when her father and I divorced." She looked up; the women at a nearby table were unabashedly staring. "Besides, I have to admit, I thought it would make things safe. If one of her escapades got into the paper, Jenna Walsh, who would know that was Maxine Hammond's daughter? But now you found out."

To gain time, Linda sipped her coffee. At her work, no matter how outrageous a case some client presents, it has always happened before. You can find precedents, you can grasp guidelines—there is nothing the books have not covered. But sitting here, with Maxine waiting for a response, she knew there were no guidelines. She was on her own. Flying blind. To offer sympathy for a miserable situation, and at the same time to pretend the situation was something she had known about all along: her mission.

If it worked, it was only because Maxine at this point was incapable of thoughtful analysis. Nuances escaped her, facial expression escaped her, the sardonic voice of a presumed friend escaped her. She was wrapped up in her own predicament—the predicament for which, after all her evasions, at last she had a listener.

"Did I say at eleven she rebelled? Cross that out. Anything that goes on at that age has been heralded years before—don't we know it. Of course there were signs. In fourth grade they suggested she stay back a year. A girl who tested okay, but there she was at the bottom of the class. Maybe if I'd agreed to it then—no? Wouldn't have made a difference? And she had no friends? No friends, that is, she would ever bring home. Anything she liked, it had to be private. Not to be shared with her mother. Linda, is all this boring you? Don't you have to get to work? Anyhow, those years when Bob was leaving me. I blamed myself. For not being attractive enough to hold a husband so my daughter could have a stable family."

Linda saw the woman with two children from the courthouse coming in at the door. Just the three of them, studies in stupefied fatigue. Whoever it was for whom they had gone to court, he had evidently not been released.

"Anyhow, thirteen years old, that's when she left home. Thirteen years, eleven months, five days. We've never slept under the same roof again. Oh, I don't lose track. Not completely. Sometimes I hear nothing for months, but then there's contact again. If you want to call it contact. Could be the police. She's been picked up for something. Disturbing the peace. Soliciting. I don't know. Could be the people at a drug program. I pulled every connection to get her into this good one, but after a month, she pulled out. Or could be some- one she lives with. Girl or man—never stays the same. That volatile temperament acts up and the roommate moves out. But meanwhile, she calls. She's sick, will I send money for medicine. Or they're late on the rent. Or this guy just raped her, she thought he was so nice but he raped her and now she needs money for an abortion." Maxine tore her napkin into little pieces; then she tried putting them together. "Nineteen years old and she's had three abortions. Three that I know of."

With a pointed clatter, the people at the next table got up.

"Like I said, I have these dreams. She'll turn a cor- ner. It will run its course, and suddenly she'll change. She'll decide she really wants to go to school, hold down a job, stay in a program. I dream it, but I'm no fool. I know it won't happen. Linda, don't shake your head. It can't." Maxine spoke vehemently; color crept up her pale cheeks. "Too much time has gone by. She's missed a whole stage of growing up. Adoles- cence. Something you can never recover. She has this fragile look, like a flower—you saw. But inside she's a riotous mess, she always will be."

Up front, Linda saw the waitresses in furtive conversation; they had sat too long at this table. "Maxine, I think they want us to go."

"I'll order something else. Linda, what do you
want? Ham and cheese? Chef's salad? Pecan pie? I'll
choke if I eat." The danish still lay on her plate.

Two pecan pies, Linda told the waitress. Then she
asked Maxine how she had gotten to Jay Earling.

"He was the lawyer for the Center, so I knew the
name. I called him once before and he was cheap. Half
of what the other lawyers charge. Less than half. I
guess he doesn't have such a hot practice."

She thought of that secretary knitting a blue
sweater. Not hot at all.

"That other time, the landlord wanted to evict her,
but Earling got it fixed. And this time in court, whatever he said, it worked. And he doesn't talk. He's
cheap and he doesn't talk. No one knows the truth.
Except"—Maxine looked around—"now you do."

"Maxine, you know I would never—"

"You know what really worries me? That I'll blurt
it out myself. It's always with me. Whoever is in my
office, Joyce is the one I'm seeing. Her long hair, her
hollow cheeks, that blank stare she gives me. Crazy,
isn't it? I'm concentrating on a girl, genuinely trying
to help her, and I think what right do I have. Advis-
ing this girl when I could never do a thing with my
own, I ruined her. Maybe I should do the decent thing
and quit."

Now at least she had something valid to say. Maxine was all wrong. In the first place, the failure was not on her. It was something inborn, perhaps genetic—at any rate, a failure for which she can't possibly hold herself responsible. And in the second place, Maxine should not for a moment think of quitting. She has a real contribution to make. The Center is lucky to have her.

It was time for her question. Why did Maxine go to see Marylou?

"You know about that? It was one of those times when I had no idea where she was. You can't imagine what it's like. A month goes by, two months—you have horrible dreams, your heart stops each time the phone rings. So I seized on Marylou because I'd once seen them together. I went into a store and there they were. Joyce and Marylou, being chummy. Don't ask me what the connection was. Those girls—the lines form and break, form and break. At that time, Marylou seemed a rock of stability. Someone who lived in a regular house, went to school, had a parent in attendance. So I tried—went and asked did she know anything. Shameless. And it did no good. If she knew, she wasn't telling."

Maxine had eaten her pie, Linda saw. She was feeling better, Maxine said. A relief, after all the months of control, being able at last to talk. It's been a big help, yes, she does feel better.

Maxine felt better, she felt worse. What an error! To think that Maxine—Maxine and Jay Earling—were in a scheme to sell babies. A scheme that could even involve murder. Because of dumb luck that she didn't deserve, Maxine had been too overwrought to apply logic to Linda's misguided questions, hadn't even thought to inquire what Linda was doing at the courthouse on this particular morning. But suppose she had known! It just showed what pits you could fall into when suspicion became your natural habitat.

Maxine should go on without her, she said when they got to the street. No, not back to the office, she was taking the day off. Day off: she heard the light free sound of it. A lie. She had no plans. When she got into her car, she turned left only because the car in front was going that way. She thought she might drive till her gas ran out, but instead she headed for the place where she got her hair done. They were amazed: Miss Stewart at noon on a weekday! Yes, Bert had time, but why a haircut, she had a cut just last week, didn't she remember? She looked at a sign above the cashier's desk: Restore. A new product. She wanted a shampoo, she said. "We'll get you out fast," the girl promised: she knew her customers. "That's all right. No hurry today. And see if I can have a manicure." Fantasy. A hair wash and nail polish to restore a shattered ego.

She walked a few blocks when she got out. A fine day, but the brisk air on a scalp that had recently been warmed made her shiver. Not restored yet, obviously, and she went to the nearest phone booth. She had never called Harold at work; her fingers shook as she ruffled through the pages.

Dr. Powderly had a patient. Who should the nurse say was calling?

She could see him, his expansive shoulder bent comfortingly over someone's open mouth. And he left the patient immediately when he heard who it was. "Linda, I didn't want to call. I thought I'd wait another couple of days—"

"Don't wait. Come tonight."

Being with a man who cares for you, who will drop everything to be with you—what better restorative than that? She might have thought of it before she spent all that money at the beauty parlor. But no, she was glad to have her hair soft and fluffed, to see him look approvingly at her hands when she laid them on the restaurant table. Harold always chose expensive restaurants where his affluent patients dined. A walk to their table meant, invariably, a stop at two or three other tables where those patients might be sitting. They all liked him. A dentist doesn't involve one in the unsettling intimacy engendered by a doctor; there is no unease about meeting him in public. They all liked him, they were inclined to put down their forks and exchange a few words with him, and they also were pleased to turn on the woman who was with him their considered approbation. She was obviously suitable, their glances said; sufficiently good-looking but not too young or dazzlingly attractive.

"They think you're okay," Harold said when they finally sat at their own table.

She nodded. It was unnecessary to talk much. Like a gynecologist, a dentist, a successful dentist, has to be adept at supplying the small talk to which the patient in a disheveled state can listen without having to respond—and Harold was eminently successful. She didn't in the least love him—she could never love anyone whose ideas hewed so abjectly to the standards of others—but she enjoyed him, she lapsed readily into contentment with him. Facing Harold across the white tablecloth, she felt herself enveloped by the serenity she'd been hoping for since noon.

It lasted, that serenity, till he drove her home. He turned off the motor and looked at her. He would come in, he often did. She never objected, why should she?—he was a considerate lover. But he was also a man of ritual, and the ritual of lovemaking is the first thing to be impaired if there is a baby in the house. During the last five months, she had felt the edginess gather in him at countless times. When she paid the baby-sitter—didn't just pay her but found herself engaged in the compelling talk about feedings, routines, disposition, weight. When she went in to check on the baby herself—a check that because of the curve of Elena's cheek against the sheet or the angle of two bent legs sometimes took longer than the promised couple of minutes. And of course when a noise from the nursery caused an interruption. Once when all had seemed settled with the two of them, the baby uttered a sharp cry. Just one, but she jumped up. Choking, she thought. Suffocation. Crib death. "I'll be right back," she said. "Wait." She was in fact back within two minutes, but he didn't wait. When she returned he was sitting on the edge of the bed tying his shoe.

There would be no interruptions tonight. He would not even see the carriage; she had pushed everything into that one room and closed the door. Their love-making would benefit—he must be thinking this, how could he not be. But it was what she herself could not bear; the idea that because she had lost Elena, Harold's pleasure would be greater.

She stood looking out at the wide lawn. Hers was one of this suburb's older apartment complexes. Over the years, the trees had grown to full height, the shrubbery fit with lush exactitude in its assigned beds. And the planting was artfully designed to be colorful for a good eight months; at this time of year, graceful street lights shed their glow on the yellow and bronze clusters of chrysanthemums.

Usually Harold commented on all this; he was a man to appreciate good management. "They certainly know how to take proper care of a lawn," he would say. Or, "Great the way they keep these paths in shipshape order." Or, "Take a look at those flower beds, you have to hand it to them." Tonight, however, his sturdy step moved quickly, oblivious of the well-maintained vistas. Well, why wouldn't he be in a hurry—he could figure out what was ahead as well as she could.

"Oh, Lord, it's been such a beastly day," she said.

He said anyone whose job was listening to teenagers for eight hours a day was entitled to feel low.

"Don't blame them. Most of them are good kids. I like them. It's not their fault sex is decreed for them at that crazy age, so they're lying in the back seat of cars when they might still be playing with dolls." She had meant to be very cool. A sedate mention of the control needed in her work. Nonjudgmental insights, neutrality, sympathy—all that. But suddenly she heard her own sobs. "Dolls. What am I saying? I mean babies. All that about babies. Babies they don't want or they might get rid of or they're scared Mama will find out about or they think maybe they can take care of while they finish high school. They're seventeen years old and it's up to them. They can decide. Free choice. They're in the driver's seat. No one can take anything from them if they don't want it taken."

With his sober gaze he regarded her. He might have been considering which of two alternative treatments to advise for an ailing molar. "You've had a terrible loss," at last he said.

By her silent nod, she admitted it.

"And to have to handle it all alone."

Another acquiescent nod.

"These last two days, I don't know how you got through them."

"I really didn't. I've been snapping at everyone. And this morning I did something dumb. A big lapse in judgment."

"Linda, dear, I understand. Indefensible lapses when one is troubled—I encounter the problem too. But solitude—it's a curable condition, after all. So why don't we treat it wisely. Apply the tested remedy."

She felt her heel dig into a moist spot of grass. "I guess so," she said vaguely.

A very pretty fifteen-year-old lived in the apartment across the hall from Linda, and because of the rules laid down by her unpermissive parents, this semidark spot under a tree where Harold had halted was where the girl parted at night from her boyfriend. Linda would see them sometimes, the girl at once tense and melting, the boy leaning over in a pose of helpless yearning. Because Harold was leaning over in the same way now, it suddenly struck her what he was talking about. Despite all the professional terms— "apply the tested remedy," "curable condition," "treat it wisely"—nothing to do with dentistry at all. Nothing. What new error has she made! What conviction that she can't possibly agree to has she let him seize on!

She thrashed the rejections around in her mind, trying to settle on some dignified and tactful phrasing, but when she opened her mouth, Harold was still talking. He was going to call Lenny. Lenny would be beside himself with pleasure. Lenny had been after him for years—why didn't he get married again? These young people, they had no idea of the obstacles that could be raised by age and habit and a heightened discriminatory sense.

Lenny was Harold's son in college in California; Harold had always wanted to introduce them, but somehow it had never come off. But now Lenny must be told right away, Harold said. Because of the difference in time, it was just half past six in California. Exactly when it was expedient to get him on the phone: after classes, before supper.

"But Harold, wait. I mean—"

"Oh, my dear, I know what you're thinking. He'll object, he'll say he should have had a chance to meet you first. Believe me, dear girl, that's not Lenny's way. He doesn't stand on ceremony. He's the soul of generous good nature. When I tell him about you, he'll love you sight unseen. And vice versa," he complacently added.

In his rush to strike that time between supper and study, he had already turned to leave. When he moved into the light, his large figure cast its shadow on the admirable path. "But Harold..." she said again. He was gone. He was going to give the news to his good-natured complaisant son Lenny.

ELEVEN

"LINDA, YOU DON'T LOOK too good." Fran, standing beside her desk next morning.

"I'm engaged. To be married," she flatly added.

"Harold?—oh, of course. All the best, darling."

"Fran, stop it. It's a big mistake. I couldn't collect myself to speak up, or I didn't want to hurt him or something. But I'll have to disabuse him right away. It's impossible. Out of the question."

Fran, who had been bending to kiss her, now moved away. "The one time I met him, he seemed very—"

"Nice. Yes, he is. Nice, thoughtful, amiable, sympathetic." She remembered the moment last night when he obviously wanted to come in and for the most considerate of reasons decided against it. "You know, there are two kinds of dentists. One goes on drilling till you're frantic, you think one more second of that torture and you'll pass out, so you wriggle your toes and squeal, and he turns off the drill. The second one turns it off before the frenzy sets in: he's in there feeling with you. He says, Suppose we take a little rest. All I mean is, I'd recommend him any day for a dentist." She looked down at her mail: a newsletter about teen-age sexuality being offered at bargain prices. "Also, he's a great date for maybe once a week. Someone to eat with, talk to, go to bed with. But marry him! God, no."

Confronted with this outburst, Fran was silent a minute. Then she said she was surprised he had not asked Linda before.

"Actually he'd been working up to it. From a dozen signs, I felt sure he was working up to it. But then the baby. Oh, he didn't exactly say he didn't like babies. He'd listen politely when I said how beautiful she was, or how bright, or what sensational new stage she was up to. But he never made an effort to be with her. It was plain he had no desire to share his life with a child. But now..."

"Now that the baby's gone," Fran quietly finished.

"In my mind it would always be a kind of trade-off. Elena for Harold—as if a perverse fate had arranged it. I had to lose the child to get the man."

"Linda, that's too—"

"Irrational. I know. I sound like our teenagers. Imaginary fears. But still it's the way I'd see it. An exchange. Maybe I'd even blame him. I know he had nothing to do with my losing that child, but in bad moments I'd con myself into thinking he did." She threw the newsletter into the trash basket. "Anyhow, I don't want to marry him. Period. I'm not going to."

"Well, honey, if you're sure."

When Fran left, she settled down to her clients. The first was a boy who needed help in telling his girl-friend he couldn't see her while he was studying for finals. The second was a girl who needed help in telling her boyfriend she wanted an abortion. The third was a girl from Plains High School. Plains High: where Marylou had gone. Leave it to Fran, Linda thought as the girl walked in. Kimberly, her name was. Kimberly Lang. Perhaps, plucking that name out of the pile, savoring the glossy syllables, her parents had envisioned a child to match it. Someone graceful, sweet-tempered, lithe. They could not have pictured the girl who shuffled into the room, turned to go out, came unwillingly in again, said finally she didn't know why she was here.

"Why did you come, Kimberly?"

"My guidance counselor said I should."

"Maybe we could talk a little about why you think your counselor made the suggestion."

Kimberly said she was all right. She was doing fine. It was just she wasn't sleeping. She couldn't fall asleep, and when she did, she'd wake a couple of hours later. Just lie there awake, at like three o'clock. "Oh, well, I don't care," she said.

"Kimberly, you seem to be sad about something. What is it you don't care about?"

"I told you, it doesn't matter." The girl sat looking at her shoes. "Oh, well. I missed two periods. But maybe it's a mistake. Yeah, I guess a mistake," her droning voice protested.

"It might be a mistake, I agree. I'll give you an address so you can have a reliable test. But let's suppose you are pregnant. I'd like to know your thoughts about the whole thing."

The girl slumped back. Her gaze was still on her legs, those unhelpful appendages. "My mother will kill me," she said.

Sometimes Linda thought, I could sit here without saying a word, all I'd need would be a box programmed with the appropriate responses. My mother will kill me: push button A. I don't care: button B. My boyfriend says not to worry: button C. Then she would be ashamed of this thought; she would tell herself each client demanded unique handling, you simply had to find wherein the uniqueness lay.

"When you say your mother would kill you, what do you mean?"

"She wouldn't really. Not kill." Kimberly hunched lower in her chair. "But she'd be angry. She'd scream and cry at once. That's what she does. Maybe I won't tell her."

Button D: it rippled out. The changes in one's body. The clothes beginning to be tight. The difference between coming out with the truth now or waiting till the parents perceive it on their own. The question which of the two courses would have the better results.

"Kimberly, you seem to be going through a lot right now. What do you see as your choices?"

More slouching. She wouldn't have an abortion, not ever, she was too scared. Her girlfriend had one, and she had a bad time.

"Well, what kind of discussion have you had about this with your boyfriend?"

Oh, him. He's all right. He's generous. He buys her lots of things.

"Have the two of you really talked about what having a baby would mean?"

"He takes me to the movies and stuff. He says we could use that money for the baby. So I shouldn't worry."

Linda averted her head for a second. Cheap comfort: we could teach that boyfriend a thing or two. "I hear you say he reassures you. But it sounds as if you still are worrying. You're not convinced there'd be enough money to take proper care of a child."

"Oh, money." Suddenly a vibrant voice issuing from the lethargic face. "That's all we talk about at home. Where's the money coming from, where's the money coming from. All my mother ever says, every single day. I don't want it to be like that with me. I want some way to get money. Like that girl."

"What girl?"

"The one who died." Abashed at her own outbreak, Kimberly resumed her slump.

"Kimberly, what girl? Do you mean Marylou?" Linda said sharply.

"She sat next to me in study hall last year. We were in the last row. We could do our nails and the teacher wouldn't see."

"What about Marylou and money? Kimberly, tell me." A mistake—her urgent voice, her severe gaze.

This was the room in which you said, Suppose we talk a little about your problem, or, You don't seem to feel very good about your choices. That whole laid-back approach, suggesting, coaxing, paraphrasing, but never demanding or domineering. Kimberly would be within her rights to clam up.

Kimberly did in fact close her lips. Then she sighed and said she'd met Marylou the day before she died. "Was killed, I should say. She was with this girl with red hair and a yellow jacket. I told her I thought I was pregnant, so then she did a little jig. Right in front of Wallach's drugstore. 'Be like me,' she said. 'I had a baby and tomorrow I'll be rich.'"

"Rich!" Another blunder. The girl recoiled. Forget that she said that. She doesn't want any trouble with the police. That's all she needs, along with everything else. For the police to come around. Because she doesn't know anything. She swears to God she doesn't. Marylou just said that, and then she and the other girl walked away. And she hardly knows Marylou. Just because you sit next to someone in study hall.

"Kimberly, no one's going to ask you questions. No one will come to your house. I just wonder if you know the name of the girl Marylou was with."

"I forget. Something funny. Starts with a G or J."

"Was it Jenna?"

"Jenna. Now I remember."

She got herself under control. She brought the conversation back to Kimberly, to the options—all unsatisfactory, but you don't say that—among which

Kimberly could choose, and she suggested another appointment, after the results of the pregnancy test were in.

Did she redress it? Not quite. She can't pretend she kept to the basic rule of counseling, which is to keep the counselor's own concerns under cover. Clients first. For a minute back there, Kimberly had not been first. It was Linda's concerns that had been out on the table. Kimberly may not have recognized them, but she reacted to them. Linda Stewart did that: made of a muddled teenager a creature more scared than when she came in.

Maybe this is the real price to be paid for sleuthing. Not the travail that goes with concealment, the disciplined effort of pursuit. It's rather the sense that your personality must change as you go in for unprecedented actions. Thoughtlessness, callousness, trickery. You ignore principles. You hurt people. You take on a new character, and not in the least an attractive one.

And she's not ready to stop yet. Maxine was on the phone when she came in, but Linda waited, a stubborn figure in the doorway. "Maxine, do you know where Jenna is? Joyce. I'll explain in a minute."

Maxine's head jolted toward the door. Who was passing? Who could hear? "Actually, I do know. She's a waitress at the Golden Parrot. That's one of the clubs on Lancaster. At least she was doing that last week. Sometimes she holds a job as long as four weeks. Sometimes not. Linda, what—"

"Listen. You know about my suspicion: Marylou had been offered money for the baby, and that's why she asked for her back. The police don't agree, but I still think it. Anyhow, a girl was just in my office..." She told it quickly, the words filtered through her ardor. "So that's it. I want to ask your daughter. Assuming she was the one with Marylou. What did Marylou mean by saying she'd be rich tomorrow? Who was going to pay her off? What's the story?"

Maxine stroked the collar of her blouse. "You want to go to Joyce? Get her at work?"

"I wouldn't mention you, of course."

"You wouldn't have to. She'd know. Someone from her mother's office—you really think she wouldn't know? Linda, I understand what you're going through. But Joyce—for her to find out I spy on her. You know how I found out where she works? I waited five nights. Five nights, me alone on a dark corner. And then I won't even say what I did to see what was going on inside. The subterfuges. The indignity. Peering in at windows." When she paused, Linda couldn't help marveling. Maxine was considered quiet by the rest of the staff. When they went out to lunch, she was the one who silently nodded. Nice but passive, was the verdict. But get her on the subject that tore at her heart, and the words were there. An explosion of them, steaming, unstoppable.

"If she knew all this, it would finish us. The thread is so tenuous anyhow. At least if she's in trouble, bad trouble, she lets them call me. But she could break even that. She could throw over everything just to get out from under my prying eyes. You don't know what damaging acts she's capable of.''

Oh, God, she had hurt someone else.

''Besides, if you somehow got past that. She'd never talk to you anyhow. You'd still be a middle-aged woman. Her mother's generation. She doesn't talk to people of her mother's generation. They're the enemy.''

''Oh, Maxine . . .''

''If you knew someone her own age. Someone you could trust. Someone savvy enough to get around her, and also reliable enough not to blow it.'' Maxine looked up. Did Linda know a young person like that?

''Never mind, Maxine. Forgive me for messing things up.''

Yes, definitely a hurt to Maxine, for whom the image of her daughter would now loom in more wounding colors than ever. Linda walked back to her own office. Forgive me, she had said, but the fact was, she'd do it again. Do the unforgivable, keep on doing it. Trickery, callousness, betrayal, till she found out what she was after.

TWELVE

THE PHONE WAS RINGING when she opened the door to her apartment. "Linda, am I ever glad I got you."

"Hello, Harold."

"I was counting on tonight, so much to talk about."

"Actually, I want to talk to you too," she said.

"It has to wait. I just heard from my father. His housekeeper, that is. He's had another heart attack. His heart, you know."

She ought to know; he talked about it often enough—his elderly but active father who lived somewhere in the Midwest and had already had two heart attacks, for both of which Harold had been in anxious attendance. He was a conscientious son, as he had been a conscientious husband. It was the way he'd been described to her a year ago by a friend. "You'll like him, Linda. His wife just died after one of those dragged-out illnesses. Pain, remission, hope, despair—the usual." How long ago had that been, Linda asked. "Almost six months. And he's coming for dinner tonight, this paragon, so you should wear something snappy." "Just half a year? Last thing he'll want is to have another woman thrown at him." "Don't you believe it. That's when they're most vulnerable. They've just lost a good thing—in his case it was twenty-two years of a good thing—and what they want is to duplicate it. They're devastated about the dead wife and desperate for someone to replace her.''

The friend had it right. From their first date, Harold had made clear where he was heading. It took him a while, he was deliberate as well as conscientious, but last night he had the proposal. And tonight she had been planning to disabuse him. ''…leaving on a seven-thirty plane,'' he was saying.

''You really have to go?''

He was surprised. Of course he had to. He hated it more than she did. Leaving on just the night when … well, just tonight. But he was lucky to get a seat at the last minute. His suitcase is packed. A car is meeting him at the other end. He should be at the Cardiac IC unit by midnight. Please God it's not too late.

You can't tell a man who is rushing for a Cardiac IC unit that you prefer not to marry him. ''Bad timing,'' she said.

''Worse than you know. Lenny came in.''

''Lenny?''

''I called him last night. And that boy, what do you think he did. Got on the red-eye, stumbled in at seven this morning. I'm delighted to see him, but I don't know. When I was in college we never dreamed of missing a class. Sore throat, broken leg, mono—there we were, taking notes. He says classes are the least. Well, he's a smart kid, I guess he knows what he's talking about.''

She mumbled an assent.

"Have to run. Linda, I'll call you."

When she hung up, she walked around the apartment. The door to the baby's room was closed, a useless closing, because imagination gave her a precise picture of its contents. First the crib with those riotous bumpers, and next to that the carriage with the gaudy rattles tied to one side, and next to it an old suitcase in which Claudette said she had managed to put all the clothes, and over that the pink blankets, and finally, in a box, the toys. The toys it had been her exquisite pleasure to select. Some child would be beautifully endowed. However, it is never as easy to give things away as you expect. We certainly can use it, they say at the church. We'll send someone over as soon as we get a chance. But they don't get a chance that day or the next, someone's van needs a new transmission, how about Friday at the latest? And meanwhile the stuff is here. Glaring at you through the door. Tearing at your heart. The bounty that Lady Bountiful does not seem able to dispose of.

She walked into the kitchen, she was taking chips out of the freezer when the intercom rang. "Leonard Powderly," a voice said. "Harold's son."

"Well, Lenny. Come on up."

One of the advantages of apartment living. You have time to brace yourself. Harold's son. He would be as conscientious, as affable and sweet-tempered as his father. He must be; look at the way he had come on the run to celebrate his father's supposed engagement. She would not reveal the truth. She would simply accept his good wishes and send him on. She left the chops on the table and went in to comb her hair.

Eighteen years old, a great student, but emotionally on the immature side, Harold had said about his son. But when Lenny came up, she saw that Harold hadn't told the whole story. Nothing to account for the youthful scowl, the censorious gaze, the whole air of being on a distasteful assignment. Faces like that can be a token of adolescence, of a time when every new encounter can seem portentous and every change must be for the worse. "I guess you're Miss Stewart," he said.

Miss Stewart: okay, if that's what he wants to call her. She asked him to come in.

"I thought, since my father's away, we could have a chance to talk," his stiff voice said.

Another anomaly. In her office, she's the one to put in a plug for conversation. "I thought we might talk about why you're upset." "Maybe we should talk further about these particular fears." She said it would be nice to talk to him.

He sat on the front half of the only straight-backed chair. "I'm not sure how well you know my father."

She said they'd seen each other a couple of times a week for almost a year.

"Sometimes you can't tell about a person from just going out on dates with him."

She said she'd be the first to agree.

"My father's a complicated man, Miss Stewart. Also, a rigid one. He likes things to be exactly the way he's ordered them."

Familiar ground now; she could speak more freely. His father is what? Forty-nine? And Lenny is eighteen. Across a gap like that, the older generation often seems rigid; it's not uncommon.

"It's not him and me. We have things worked out; we did that long ago. It's you, Miss Stewart. I don't know whether you'd be able to accommodate."

"I see."

"For instance, vacations," the boy said in his sententious voice. "Maybe he didn't tell you, but he goes on a fishing trip every spring. He's very serious about it. The guide, the equipment, the territory, the maps. A man's trip, of course."

"Of course."

"And every summer, a climbing expedition. Not just small mountains. Rugged trips, six, seven days. We usually go to the Sierras but next summer we plan on further north." He squirmed on the edge of his chair. "It's not something a novice could undertake. You have to train for a long time."

"Sounds impressive."

"It means a lot to my father. We've been doing it for years."

"Lenny, can I give you something to drink? A coke? Coffee? Beer?"

It didn't help. "Housekeeping," the boy went on. "He has finicky habits. My mother knew exactly how to take care of him; she didn't mind catering to his little whims.''

"Lucky man, your father."

"It wasn't luck that she died," he said. "That was a terrible blow. It left him demolished. Everyone said it."

"Exactly what did everyone say?"

He took a deep breath; someone gearing himself for the big dive. "That he wouldn't be able to make any sensible decisions for at least two years. That he shouldn't try to. He wouldn't be in proper shape."

When he stopped talking, she heard the elevator door open; the couple across the hall were coming home. "Lenny, have you discussed any of this with your father?"

It was why he had come in such a hurry, he said.

"You were going to tell your father he wasn't in proper shape to decide about getting married?"

"I'm not the only one who thinks it. One of his brothers does. My mother's sister. His best friend."

She stood up. When she moved into this two-bedroom apartment from her old one downstairs, the living room turned out to be larger as well; her furniture didn't fill it. The coffee table looked inadequate; another chair was needed next to the couch; the space on the opposite wall could use a bookcase. Little by little, she had thought. First the baby.

"It's you I'm thinking of too," he said, and ran his tongue around his lips. Foolish boy: a drink would make it easy for him. Even if he didn't touch a sip, something to press against his dry mouth or hold in his hand. His hand which, she saw, was shaking. "I didn't think I'd have a stepmother. Anyhow, not so soon," he said.

Well, there it was. She was not Miss Stewart, who lacked the expertise to undertake a six-day mountain climb, or who might not give her full attention to catering to a man's whims. She was the stepmother. At a boy's time of greatest stress, greatest need for the semblance of independence, someone to cast him as a dependent. Someone to barge in, give orders, set limits, propose goals. It was admittedly worse when the child being barged in on was an adolescent—and Lenny was still very much in the clutches of adolescence. From where he was sitting, Linda constituted an invasion. A person to have power over him without having done anything to deserve it. That was the thing about stepparents. They were granted the privilege without having run the course. They got to have parental authority though they had never paid the parental dues.

Linda looked at the boy whose glasses had slipped off and whose scowl had broken apart, leaving only an uneasy blankness. She wanted to tell him that his fears were all wrong and also that they were wholly justified. Also, she suddenly wanted something else.

"Lenny, listen. Did your father tell you about me?"

"He said you worked in this agency where you advise kids what to do."

"Actually, the last thing we do is give advice. What we want is to strengthen their insights so they can make the decisions for themselves. But that's not what I mean. Did he tell you what happened? That I adopted a child and two days ago the biologic mother took it back?"

He mumbled an assertion of regret.

"Come in here. I want to show you something." So she was opening that door after all. The stuff was less orderly than she remembered. The crib bumpers were on the floor, the clowns and animals in a gaudy tangle of fluff. The suitcase was open—did Claudette leave it open?—to show the pile of stretchies and sweaters and shirts. The carriage had slid to the other side of the room. Also, in that image she carried in her head, she had forgotten the rubber bathtub, the half-finished box of diapers, the bottles, the miniature spoon.

But she knew what impression she was after, and here she had it. A panorama of devastation. A visual demonstration of loss. Equipment, had he said? Let him beat this for equipment that translates into caring, into seriousness, into dedication.

"All that? Tough," he said without irony.

"Doubly tough, really"—she closed the door—"because both of them were murdered after I gave the baby back. The girl and the baby."

"Jesus."

"So now I don't believe the girl, the birth mother, meant what she said. That she wanted the baby for herself."

"You think it was some kind of scam? Is that it?"
Without that cultivated sternness, his face looked
younger. She could see the relationship to Harold. The
Harold who radiated feelings of warmth and gal-
lantry when he stopped at the tables of his patients.

"That's what I think. Her scam or someone else's."
She waited another minute while someone else got out
of the elevator and jangled keys in the hall outside.
"Anyhow, this afternoon I got wind of something. A
girl saw Marylou—that's the mother—the day before
she asserted her rights to the baby. And what Marylou supposedly said—let me get it right—she said,
'Look at me, I had a baby and tomorrow I'll be rich.'
My informant knows nothing else. Just that one possibly telling quote. But there was another girl with
Marylou. A friend. And she might be able to tell us
more."

"So ask her."

"It's not so simple. I know who the girl is: Jenna
Walsh. But she's the kind who won't give an adult the
time of day. Especially not an adult who might be
connected to her mother. She's a year older than
you—nineteen—and she may well be on drugs, and
she's in trouble with the police on and off. Also she
hasn't lived home or gone to school for years."

"One of those," Lenny dismissively said. He might
not feel tolerance—who does at eighteen?—but he had
perception. He had placed the girl.

He had also jumped to the next step. He said if she
wouldn't mind, he'd have that drink now—yeah, a

coke would do fine—and when she came back from the kitchen, he said could he help.

"Lenny, that's up to you."

"I mean, would you like me to try speaking to this Jenna? If you thought it would do some good."

She watched him finish half the coke in one gulp. She had done it. His father's rashness was erased, the stepmother menace was erased; the whole threat of demeaning change was erased; in their place was the thrill of the hunt.

"It won't be easy. She has a job as a waitress at a nightclub in Plummers Bay. A place called the Golden Parrot."

He knew it, he said. And when she looked at him, he said he remembered it from when he went to high school.

"This Jenna, she's a very troubled girl. If she even guessed that you were an emissary from her mother's colleague. That you were trying to pump her."

"Hey, you can trust me. I guess I know how to strike up a conversation without spilling the beans."

How you had to watch every word with them. "Lenny, I'm sure you do."

"So if I sort of knew what she looks like."

Linda thought of that girl who walked down the aisle of the courthouse. The practiced disdain, the stubborn detachment, the gaze that was careful not to turn to where her mother was sitting. "Red hair, lanky, thin. Undernourished, call it. And listen, Lenny. Be careful. I mean..." What exactly did she mean? He was at the door already, her new sidekick, her partner: a young man who couldn't wait to get started. She stood with him in the hall till the elevator came, murmuring something about caution, night-clubs, trouble. He didn't listen. He was a conspirator off to taste the adventure that doesn't come often and has to be grabbed peremptorily when it does.

She waited till the elevator door closed on his ex-alted look. What had she done! What had she let him in for! All she'd wanted was to wipe that sanctimoni-ous objection from his face. To cut through the pained demurrers. But it had moved so quickly to something else. His eager voice, his giddy resolve, his transfor-mation from cheeky insolence to knowing complic-ity—they seduced her. They led her on. Suddenly she'd found herself with an ally.

But now she considered. An inexperienced eigh-teen-year-old going into that club. He knew it, he'd said. Sheer bravado. The brash assertion of one whose knowledge is strictly secondhand. The moment he en-tered the Golden Parrot, he would be spotted for an outsider. Long before he found Jenna, someone would have taunted him, sparked that touchiness that could turn so readily to bellicosity. Words would ensue. Maybe something worse—from adventure to debacle in five minutes.

She ran to the window, but he was gone, of course. Only a woman walking her dog and men hurrying home from work on those well-maintained paths Harold approved of. He would not in the least approve the mission on which she had sent his innocent boy. That nice, courteous, conscientious Harold—he would be furious. He would find the whole business impossible to understand.

She hardly understood it herself. She went into the kitchen, where the chops had defrosted; too late to put them back in the freezer. But no way was she going to cook them either. The idea of actually seasoning them and slipping them under the grill and arranging them on a plate—unthinkable. But she kept sitting at the table. This must be how the parents of teenagers spend their nights, she thought. Conjuring up scenes of havoc or injury, regretting something they themselves have said, waiting for the phone call. And in her case the wait was worse. Because even if he did encounter trouble, the woman who'd sent him into it was the last one he would tell.

THIRTEEN

YOU ALWAYS WORRY about the wrong thing: something else the parents of teenagers can tell you. Lenny was at her house the next morning. She had gotten up an hour ahead of her usual time and dressed and boiled herself an egg which she then poured into the sink, and when she went down to the lobby, there he was. A tall, thin figure standing beside the copper planter.

"Lenny!"

"I didn't know what time you get up. I figured I'd better wait down here."

"I get up early," she idiotically said. "Would you like to come up for coffee?"

"No, thanks. To tell the truth, I'm going home to sleep."

"You haven't slept all night?"

"When I left that place, it was after three. And I wanted to be here at seven in case you went off."

She looked at his pale face. He must have been riding around for hours: aimless riding, the worst kind. A danger she had not even thought of. "Maybe we should sit over there."

There was a bench along the wall. He waited till she greeted someone—it was the couple in the apartment above who had given her their discarded baby things. Then he said, "She put a five-hundred-dollar deposit on a car. Marylou, I mean."

"Lenny, start from the beginning."

"That's the whole thing. Jenna told me." He spoke in a low, intense voice. "They went into an automobile showroom, Jenna and Marylou, and Marylou said, 'That car, the blue one, that's the one I want,' and she put down a deposit. Oh, I forgot, the car cost twelve thousand, five hundred. Without air conditioning."

She looked up, but he wasn't smiling. Under his bleary gaze, he was still exalted. Single-handed, he had gone into hostile territory and bested the natives and found what he was after. Mission amazingly accomplished.

"Maybe you'd better tell me everything."

He looked around the lobby, where a man had come in to water the plants. He just went to that place, he said in his new deprecatory voice. The Golden Parrot. First he sat at the bar, then he saw a girl who looked like Jenna so he went to the area she was serving. He had a sandwich and a beer and another sandwich, and each time he made a kind of joke with the girl. Then he asked could he drive her home. She said she got off at three, so he said he'd wait. That was it. No sweat.

"Did anyone hassle you?"

"Why should they?"

Why! Because you have Serious Young Student written all over you. Because you obviously didn't fit in with whatever crowd was there. Because any irritation you feel is immediately plain on your open face. And because that's what I kept imagining while I lay sleepless in my bed.

"What about Jenna? You did drive her home?"

"Yeah. But that's all she said about Marylou. I even taped it to make sure."

"Lenny! You have a tape?"

"Here it is. You don't want to hear the whole thing."

"I really do. But not in here. Let's go outside." Because each time an elevator door opened, people came out to greet her and say not a bad day for October. She led him out, to a stone bench under a tree. It was quiet; she had no trouble hearing the words when he clicked it on.

"*...not going to keep working at that crummy club forever, it's really a dump, and besides...*" The drawling voice issued clearly from the box. Then he clicked it off.

"A lot of junk in the beginning. She's a weird one, that Jenna. But nothing about Marylou till later. I'll get to that part—"

"No. I want to hear it all."

"You sure? Okay. Here goes."

"*...not going to keep working at that crummy club forever, it's really a dump, and besides they don't pay worth a damn.*"

A car was honking down by the curb, and on the path she heard a mother telling a child to come on, but the voices, Jenna's drawling one, Lenny's encouraging one, floated clearly into the cool morning air.

"Is it a dump?"

"Didn't you notice? Like a barn. And that piano. Half the time it's not even in tune."

"So what do you figure on doing?"

"I thought maybe I'd get work buying hats. You know. Be a hat buyer for one of those fancy Mayhew stores. I have a feel for hats, I really do."

"Got any training in that field."

"They're not interested in training. They want people with imagination and flair, that's what counts. Just so you aren't—"

Aren't what? She heard a blast on the horn, then the noise of an engine revving up.

". . . or maybe something in design. Like designing store windows. Someone with imagination—they're looking for that too. Once a man, he was an artist, came to my table at the club, and I told him my ideas, and he said they were really creative."

"Sounds good." Is that what Lenny said? More interference from the engine, inscribed on a tape just a few inches from it. Lenny gently tapped the machine, as if to cajole it into performing well.

". . . even my own apartment. It's a dump and my roommate doesn't help at all. But you should see the way I have it fixed up. Just if you have imaginative

ideas and a color sense, you know how to make things work. Turn left at the next corner."

Some obstructions when he turned left. "Sorry," Lenny muttered.

"Just if it wasn't such a dump. Up on the top floor, you can suffocate all summer and you freeze the minute it gets cold. Soon as I get a little money together, I'm going to look for something else. In Plains, maybe. They have some neat apartments there."

"Plains. Isn't that where she lived? The girl who was killed. I read it in the paper." When he turned, she saw the glint of satisfaction on his face. Lenny, the canny investigator, gliding nonchalantly into the crucial subject.

"Yeah. Marylou Rogin. We were friends," Jenna said in her voice of light indifference.

"Must be terrible for you. You know someone and she gets killed."

"You know what's the worst part? Thinking about that water. What she must have looked like. Sometimes when I stay in the bathtub a long time, I hate the way my fingers look, all shriveled, when I get out."

A muffled answer. "I didn't know what to say. She had me there," Lenny mildly said.

"So when did you see her last?"

"Four days ago. I just accidentally ran into her. She said she was going shopping so I said I'd go along. I thought she meant shopping for panty hose. But guess what she did."

"I give up."

"Bought a car."

"Come on."

"I mean it. There's this showroom, corner of Madison and Edgemont. She stands at the window and then she walks in. I thought she knew someone. But no. She says she wants to see a salesman. Then she opens her pocketbook. Snooty, like. Not afraid of anyone, that girl. So she pulled out some money and they were hundred-dollar bills. I swear. Five hundred-dollar bills. She says she wants to make a deposit on the blue car over there."

"What'd the salesman say?"

"He did take the bills in back, I suppose he looked to make sure they were real. They must've been real because he came back and said didn't she want to test drive the car or something. That wouldn't be necessary, Marylou said. Just make sure no one else bought it in the meantime. Tomorrow she'd be coming in to pay the rest. Only tomorrow she was dead."

"Jesus."

"I saw the price on the windshield. Twelve five. Air conditioning extra. Hey, you went too far. That house next to the corner, that's where I live."

More static from the engine, as he evidently backed up.

"You want to come in or something?" Still the drawling voice; come in, stay out, it was all the same.

"I don't think so. It's kind of late."

"Well, thanks for the ride."

On the tape, the sound of a door slamming. Then he clicked it off. That was it, Lenny said. The whole thing.

Her feet were numb; she shuffled them on the gravel path and pulled her collar around her neck. Despite her neighbors' assertions, it was no weather for sitting out. "The whole thing," she repeated—it could not be true. He had gotten half of it; an important half, but only half nonetheless. "Tomorrow I'll be rich . . ." Rich from what particular source? He had it and he'd let it slip. Linda thought of all the places where he might have steered the flow of that frail narrative. He hadn't used them. He'd simply accepted what was offered.

Nor did he have any idea now that he'd been amiss. The self-congratulatory air remained as he leaned confidentially toward her. "Listen. My father. He's not as rigid as I said. Those climbing expeditions—anyone could come. Even someone who'd never been climbing before."

He was apologizing for the wrong thing. "Lenny, relax. I would never put on hiking shoes. I think it's barbaric to sleep outdoors. I don't walk up a hill if I can help it."

"Those trips," he said doggedly. "He just does it out of frustration."

His father frustrated? She said she would never guess it.

"Oh, he is, he surely is. It's being a dentist."

"I thought he loved it."

"He's good at it," Lenny said. "That's not the same thing."

She looked at him. Wisdom from an eighteen-year-old, at seven thirty in the morning.

"He'd really like to be a scientist. Someone in a white coat making great discoveries—you don't know about that?"

She really doesn't.

"Something about isolating the virulent factors of streptococcus mutans in saliva—that's his current dream. Maybe I don't have it exactly right, but you get the general idea. My dad's idea of heaven—him alone for ten hours a day with a hundred test tubes of saliva. One of these years, he says he'll do it. Tell his patients good-bye, lock his office, take up residence in some lab."

"I see."

"But don't worry, not right away," he said quickly. "Not till he can afford it."

She stared at the boy, his face pale from strain and excitement both. To do her honor, he had divulged the great family secret. He had made up for that sour entry into her life. And she couldn't disabuse him. Couldn't explain that since she didn't intend to marry his father, any reassurance about money was not needed.

She couldn't criticize him either. No way she could break the bubble of elation that hung around Harold's son. In fact, he was even now pointing out his insights. "That Jenna. Those delusions. A girl who did not go to high school, has no training at all, but she's going to get a job as a hat buyer. Or designing store windows. Or she'll make some money and get a nice apartment. What a weirdo. I've been taking a course in psychology this year and she exactly fits one of the types we studied. No hold on reality. Grandiose expectations. Empty inside. Emotionally labile— that means mood swings," he tolerantly explained. "One week you read about it in a book, and there she is, sitting next to you while she blabs away. It's uncanny."

No, impossible to spoil his pleasure. He had made the great discovery: life matches the textbook. By purest accident, he had found in the outside world the validation of what he learned in the classroom—she can't impair the joy of that revelation. He had hacked his way through to the treasure and come back empty-handed, and it's incumbent on her to refer only to his discernment and daring.

After he left, she drove to the police station, and Lieutenant Wilkerson turned out also to be an early riser. Yes, Miss Stewart, please come in.

The signs were still in a pile on his desk—for which Saturday was that *No Parking* stipulated? He was glad to see her, he said. He hoped she hadn't been going to any empty houses.

She said she'd gone nowhere, but she did in fact know something. That Marylou went with a friend to an automobile showroom the day before she was killed. Does he want to hear about that?

When he said he certainly wanted to hear, she was conscious of the edge of triumph in her voice. "Marylou looked at a blue car she liked and peeled off five hundred dollars as a deposit. I guess the bills were okay, not fake or anything, because the salesman asked didn't she want a test drive. Marylou said no, that didn't matter. Just she wanted to be sure no one else got it before tomorrow when she came back with the rest of the money. Another twelve thousand. Twelve without air conditioning."

Wilkerson gave his judicious nod. Then he said it jibed with what they knew. The salesman had recognized the picture of Marylou in the newspaper and had contacted them.

"Christ. You sat here all the time and didn't say a word. Why didn't you stop me?"

"I wanted to see if your information was the same as ours."

"And was it?"

"Yes."

She sat back to catch her breath. The door to the office was half open, but it was quiet in the large room beyond. No handcuffed prisoners, no phones jangling, no bustle. Evidently, if you wanted an undisturbed talk with a policeman, eight in the morning was your time.

She said the scene in the showroom wasn't the whole story.

"Let's have the rest, Miss Stewart."

"I heard this from a client who came to the office yesterday. A young girl who's upset at finding herself pregnant. She ran into Marylou on that same day and blurted out her problem, and Marylou comforted her. She said—well, here it is. I wrote it down. 'Look at me. I had a baby, and tomorrow I'm going to be rich.'"

Wilkerson tapped his pencil on the desk. "Interesting," he said.

His composed manner, his neutral tone, his air of seeing two sides to every question. "Oh, my God. I come with a story—no, two stories—about a girl who's just been killed, and all you say is interesting. Isn't it obvious from this that Marylou wasn't involved with that hypothetical drug gang of yours, that the money has to be connected with the baby?"

"I don't know. Could be that Marylou was simply offering generalized comfort to your little client. I wasn't there, of course, didn't hear the inflections, but seems to me she could have been saying, Look at me, I had a baby and it didn't spoil my life, in fact tomorrow, because of some connections I've been able to make in the high school locker rooms, I expect to come into a mint."

He was good, she had to admit. He didn't significantly alter his voice or go in for coy postures, but Marylou was suddenly evoked. The bristly hair, the jutting breasts, the sturdy arrogance.

Then he leaned forward. "Believe me, Miss Stewart, we take your ideas seriously. You think Marylou's expectation of that money has to mean someone had offered to pay her for the child? That kind of scam?''

Scam: the same word Lenny had used. "Or maybe a scam Marylou thought up herself," she said slowly.

"I assume you're thinking of the Hildebrands," he said with no expression.

"Listen. Mr. Hildebrand sort of went wild when I talked about his son. About anything that might jeopardize his precious son." "Precious:" now *she's* saying it. "Suppose Marylou did go to them. Suppose she said something like, Here's your grandchild, pay up or everyone will know...."

"So you now believe—"

"Don't keep asking me what I believe. First you tell me not to ask questions. Then you want my ideas. You're the policeman. You have all those detectives and laboratories and up-to-date machines—why don't you solve it!"

He didn't react. He didn't take offense. He must have outrage hurled at him in this office all the time. He said she could help them if she could give them two names. First, the pregnant girl who elicited the crucial comment from Marylou.

"She doesn't know anything except that one sentence she told me. I tried and tried, but that's it. Besides, she's a scared girl. Scared to have an abortion, scared to not have an abortion, scared that her mother will find out, scared that she won't, scared that her boyfriend won't help... Leave her out of it."

"How about the other one? The friend who was allegedly with Marylou in the car showroom."

She remembered what Maxine had said: Inside she's a riotous mess, she always will be. "I have to speak to someone," Linda said. "Someone close to her. If this person says it's okay—"

"I thought you were so anxious."

"Oh, I am. I am." But the matter had strayed so far afield, gone such a distance from a baby in a white coverall with red dots, that for a second she was unable to assign a shape to the particular anxiety that was driving her.

FOURTEEN

A HALF HOUR LATER she called him with the name. Jenna Walsh, also her address, also the place where she worked. "The woman said okay," she told Wilkerson.

It was not quite accurate. What Maxine had said was, "Oh, for God's sake, how can I refuse. No, it won't upset her. She's had plenty of dealings with the police for a lot worse reasons. Worse for her, I mean. It just upsets me. Something else to add to the list."

That bitter face, above the drab mannish collar—it stayed with her all morning. She was writing a report for the directors' meeting next week, and there were some very thin lines you had to tread. You painted adolescent sexuality in all its flaming and aching colors, and at the same time you made sure the colors were not too lurid. You showed that your clients were in need of special help, and also that they were like the girl or boy next door. You delineated family instability, while also making a case for parental caring. Finally, you counteracted the misperception that because you didn't specifically tell teenagers not to, you were in effect telling them how to.

At twelve thirty she told Fran she couldn't go out to lunch. At one, she ate the yogurt someone had in a

desk. At two, she took an aspirin to ward off a headache. At two thirty, the phone rang. Wilkerson. "Miss
Stewart, I'm afraid I have some bad news about that
young—"

The door opened. Maxine burst in. Maxine with
eyes wild, face distorted. "You had to go meddling,
didn't you? Couldn't just let it rest."

"Maxine?" She got up and closed the door.

"Not as if anything you'd was going to bring your
baby back. So what was it for, this aimless prying?
What's the purpose? To satisfy your curiosity? Find a
culprit? Or maybe to inflict punishment. Yes, that's it.
You're God, you can see that whoever did it gets
properly punished."

She was aware of two things simultaneously. One,
that she had put her finger down on the phone, cutting off Wilkerson's somber voice, and two, that tears
were running down Maxine's face at the same time as
she bellowed out the words.

"Besides, where'd you get the right? You think because you lost a child? Dear God, what kind of child-
raising had you put in? Six months? Five? That's what
you think qualifies you for motherhood? Entitles you
to suffer? My God. You don't know what suffering is.
You never sponged her off because her temperature
was a hundred and five and she might get convul-
sions. You didn't comfort her because her best friend
in third grade had a slumber party and didn't invite
her. You never sat by a window with your blood run-

ning cold because it was four o'clock and she wasn't home yet. You a mother! Don't make me laugh.''

Maxine did laugh—a pained guffaw emerging from her twisted mouth. ''Why'd you get mixed up with her anyhow? With both of us. Poking into our lives. Asking questions. What were you doing in court? Yes, now I think about it, I really wonder. What business of yours was it? Didn't you know it would lead to this?''

The phone rang again. She lifted the receiver, said, ''Call you later,'' hung up. Then she stood. ''Oh, Maxine. Oh, my dear.''

''You don't even know her,'' Maxine said in a new voice. ''She had such talents when she was growing up. And she was beautiful. Everyone thought she was beautiful. God. You should have seen her as a child. Those eyes, and the high cheekbones and the red hair hanging down. People would look after her in the street.''

It was the past tense that did it. The past tense with its inexorable finality. What a way for death to announce itself. A hint, an insidious whisper, a furtive intimation. Linda put an arm about the shaking shoulders beside her.

''She had so much going for her. All she had to do was reach out and grab it. She might have done that. Might have made a life for herself. It happens. They throw away six or ten or twenty years, and then, a miracle, they stop short. They stop being angry. Find something to hang onto. That was going to happen to

Joyce. That girl, she was going to be a real person after all.''

When Maxine leaned forward, she knocked over the
ceramic jug with its pile of pencils; they rolled with
quiet thuds across the desk.

"No. That's not true. I know it. She was too far
gone. You'd never believe the kind of help she's had.
It was all no use. Nothing ever took. I know what was
ahead. She'd just have kept going, down, down,
down. You think they've hit bottom but it turns out
there's always something worse.''

Linda laid her hand on Maxine's arm.

"This way it's a relief. I'll never again have to jump
when I hear the phone in the middle of the night. My
heart won't stop each time an ambulance goes by. I
can go off for a weekend without worrying what vile
thing is happening to her now. Isn't that funny,''
Maxine said. "My daughter had to die so I'd have
peace at last.''

"Maxine, sit here.''

"God, I loved her. She would never believe it. She
had no capacity for believing anyone could love her.
No trust at all. But it was true. All the misery she
caused me, it just made me love her more. She was my
baby. My only one. I have to go now and identify my
only child.''

Identify: that word out of the official terminology,
carrying all the impermissible questions. When? How?
Where? In that unspeakable manner, so the only
service left is the chilling one of identification?

"Maxine, let me come with you. To the... I mean..."

"No. I'm better off alone. I'd just go on and on like this. She would have been better, she would have got worse—all that useless speculation. And Linda, listen"—as she was going with her convulsed face out the door—"What I said about your meddling, it being your fault—that was crazy. It had nothing to do with you, I know that. Whatever you did or didn't do, it was going to happen. That was my Joyce. Always in the wrong place at the wrong time. Just cross out all the things I—"

"Maxine, dear, hush." When the door was closed, she put the pencils back in their cup. Then she called Wilkerson.

"Miss Stewart, I guess you heard. Yes, this morning. No, it would not have made a difference if you'd given us her name earlier; we would not in any case have got there before noon. What happened? She evidently came in after three this morning; her roommate was there, and the two of them stayed up for about an hour. That roommate—her name is Gail— looks to be an even worse case than Jenna. At about eight this morning Gail went out, and she came back while we were there. All she could tell us was that Jenna had been talking about some way she was going to get money. Something she knew so someone would give her money—I agree, sounds like a spot of blackmail. Cashing in, that foolhardy girl, trying to cash in on her jaunt with Marylou. Oh. Shot. A clean shot, right in the heart. And no one to hear anything, four other apartments in the house, but the people all at work. I wish I could give you more information, Miss Stewart, but we're in the dark, same as you.''

However, under that unhelpful candor, he was a good man, a kind one; he wouldn't leave it at that. ''Such a rotten end for a sorry life,'' he said. ''I understand her mother works at your agency. Poor woman. I don't know where she can find her comfort.''

She sat with her eyes closed after she hung up. Then she stood and started dusting her books. She had no rag, so she took the box of tissues she kept in her desk drawer. You were supposed to handle books gently, a delicate pressure from the sides to dislodge them, but she ignored this. *Teenage Sexuality in a Changing Society:* she put a finger behind the vulnerable place at the top of the spine and yanked. She was not delicate about the dusting either. *Psychotherapy for Adolescents:* she rubbed hard across the top, then banged the book on the desk so another cloud of dust rose up. *Conflict and Growth in the Adolescent Years:* its cover resisted her touch, so she squeezed the binding and gave a hefty pull. The book came, but it also tore. She had not quite finished one shelf when she saw the tissue was used up; the tissue she keeps to give to her young clients if they start to cry. What are their tears about anyhow? An unwanted pregnancy, an irate mother, an uncaring school system—puny problems.

As Maxine would say, they're not entitled to suffer, they don't know what suffering is.

The books were still piled on the floor when Debbie called from the switchboard that she had a visitor. No, not a client. A woman whose name is—she better pronounce it right—Sally Hildebrand.

"Be right out, Debbie."

Mrs. Hildebrand, all right, twisting her hands in the outer office as she said she wanted to have a little talk. If Miss Stewart could spare her a few minutes. She'd wait if Miss Stewart was busy.

"You don't have to wait. Please come in."

Mrs. Hildebrand's eyes widened at the mess of books on the floor, but she stepped over them and sat down and again twisted her hands. Then she took a handkerchief from her pocketbook and twisted that. Then she said she and her husband had talked it over and decided this was best. Her coming to see Miss Stewart. He'd have come himself if not for something urgent at the office.

Linda sat silent. She felt drained. *What do you believe, Miss Stewart?* Right now, she believes nothing. She understands nothing. She feels nothing except the grime on her hands from that savage dusting.

"In a way, Miss Stewart, you were right. About Gil, that is."

The precious son—now what? Right that Gil had fathered Marylou's child? She still didn't talk.

"You said we should ask him about a reward." Mrs. Hildebrand put the handkerchief back in her pocketbook and took out a small silver pen, which she twirled between two fingers. "He'd be in favor, of course he would. A reward to help find the murderer—Gil would be all for it. We know that now. In fact, Miss Stewart, any sum you'd like to suggest..."

She knew she was making it harder, but she still gave no answer except a slight inclination of her head.

"We got a letter from him yesterday," the thin voice said. "It came right after your visit. He'd just heard about that girl's death."

At last, something to say. "That girl has a name. Marylou Rogin," she said harshly.

"Yes." The pen twirled faster. "Someone in his college gets our local paper and showed him the clipping. That's how he found out. So, like I said, he wrote us. He said—well, wait."

Mrs. Hildebrand put aside the pen and took out an envelope and had trouble opening it and more trouble pitching her voice for reading. "'Dear Mom and Dad. Just saw the clipping about Marylou's death. What a rotten, rotten thing. Have they caught the bastard who did it? If no, maybe I can be a little help.'"

Mrs. Hildebrand looked up. She shivered. She tugged at her pearls. "All this time, he's been in touch with her. He knew about the baby. He's been writing to her."

Good for Gil, Linda started to say. Then she stopped. This woman was in pain, just as Maxine had been in pain, just as many parents who sat here were.

Her dearest assumptions had been shattered. The quiver of her hands was simply the expression of genuine pangs in her heart. Linda reached out her own hand. "You can't hold on to children," she said. "I know it sounds hard, but you can't protect them, you really have to let them go."

"He's been planning to major in political science," Mrs. Hildebrand said. "He wants to go into the foreign service."

"He'll keep on majoring in political science."

"His first paper, the professor gave him an A. He told him it was the best—carefully researched and full of fresh ideas."

Linda waited till the tears had stopped. Then she asked in what way Gil had thought he could help.

"He's been sending the girl money. All this time, when we thought . . . we just naturally assumed . . . He doesn't have that much to send. We don't believe in big allowances, his father and I. He's been working in the college cafeteria three nights a week. Since the start of the term, Gil serving in the cafeteria."

It won't hurt him. She didn't say that either.

"But last week she wrote him that she didn't need money. I guess, from the date, it was the day before she got killed. Should I read it to you?"

"Please."

Her artificial reading voice again. " 'Marylou told me I shouldn't bother sending anything this month. Maybe I wouldn't have to send it ever again. She just heard of this great way that she could come into a lot of money. Enough so she could buy a car and get away from home and find a decent job after she graduates. I have no idea what she was talking about, but it has to be connected to her death. So you'd better tell this to the police. The more they know, the sooner they'll be able to find the bastard.' ''

I would give him an A too, Linda thought. That nice, mixed-up, honorable poli sci major. Then she realized the woman was still talking. "We will go to the police. Of course we will, if we have to. But Dwight and I—we thought I should tell you first. Since you did come to us."

She thanked the woman. She said actually the police knew a payoff of some kind was involved in Marylou's death, but Gil's information should surely be given to them. Then she saw the expression on Mrs. Hildebrand's face. "Listen. There won't be any publicity about your son. I'll tell you who to speak to, and I know he'll keep it private."

"We had such a terrible night. We couldn't make up our minds. The shock, when we thought everything with the girl was behind him."

"It is behind him. He's just trying to do the decent thing."

"When you came yesterday, we really didn't know," Mrs. Hildebrand said. "We had lots of wrong ideas. We thought... if your coming was going to make trouble for Gil..."

"I had some wrong ideas too," she said slowly.

The silence this time was an easy one; when Linda saw Mrs. Hildebrand look again at the disheveled floor, she said something about housecleaning. Every once in a while in an office like this, some necessary housecleaning.

Mrs. Hildebrand nodded. She meant what she had said about contributing to the Center. From all she's heard, she knows they do an important job. Her neighbor—well, not really a neighbor, he lives a mile and a half away—is reputed to be active on their board. Claude Stanhope.

Linda said he was certainly active.

"Wonderful man. I don't know him but I once heard him speak."

"Tell me about it."

"It was our country club. We all went. We thought it would be about his trips. You know, what special things they bring to eat, where they live, what they wear. Nothing like that. It was deep scientific stuff. Heavy, heavy. But the funny thing was, he made it sound simple. Even those formulas he wrote on a blackboard—while he was talking, I understood every word. Of course a week later"—Mrs. Hildebrand looked up ruefully—"What am I saying, an hour later, I couldn't have told you what he said. None of it stuck. Not a sentence. Not a word. But while that runty little man was up there talking, it was magic. Pure magic for everyone."

Runty little man: is that what Claude Stanhope looked like?

"I take it back. Actually, not magic for everyone."

"How come?"

"His wife didn't even bother to listen. She sat there with that adorable face—that face she's so vain about—talking the whole time to someone next to her. Don't ask me why he married her. That's how it goes, I guess. The smartest men, but they can sometimes act like the biggest fools." It was a new Sally Hildebrand. Once her own troubles were out of the way, she could stop fiddling with her pearls or her pen or her hands, she could sit throwing off aphorisms about smart men—even her voice had deepened.

"If he's so—did you say runty looking? And thirty years older besides. You wonder why she married him."

"I don't wonder," Mrs. Hildebrand said. "She didn't have a penny. Ask anyone. Her father had been a train conductor—he was a regular on the eight twenty-three; all our men knew him. And after she got out of high school, she took what she could get. Salesgirl, telephone operator, receptionist—once she sat in a window demonstrating how some new slicing machine could work. So when a little piece of fluff like that gets a chance at an estate in Mayhew Gardens, and all the clothes she can put on her back, and a house full of servants..."

Little piece of fluff: from the facile way Mrs. Hildebrand said it, Linda knew it was not the first time. They would all say it, all the matrons in Mayhew Gardens about the interloper who had moved in on their special enclave. They knew how to handle some-one unworthy. They would dig up her blighted his-tory, compare notes on her squalid background, scoff at her tawdry ambitions. Sitting around the pool, while someone told yet again the story of how this unappreciative wife acted at her celebrated husband's speech, they would be indignant and also gratified, because they knew that this wife should never have been here in the first place. Linda hadn't particularly cared for Rosalie Stanhope when she heard her at the dinner, but suddenly she felt a stab of sympathy for the young woman: poor piece of fluff, in with people who understood her failings and saw through her mo-tives.

"She can't be so vain about her face. She wouldn't let a photographer take her picture."

"You must be mistaken."

"I was passing yesterday when he got thrown out of the house. He tried to snap her picture for a column about her husband's homecoming, and she smashed the film."

Mrs. Hildebrand shook her head. That was not the Rosalie she knew. The Rosalie she knew would be up front, primping and preening for every picture. Then she leaned confidentially forward. "I shouldn't talk like this."

"I won't tell anyone," Linda said. Though she would. She couldn't wait to tell Fran.

"It's not that. A friend of mine—a woman who lives just two houses away—is having delicious veal birds tonight because of one of Rosalie's servants."

"I don't get it."

"Rosalie fired them all. Cook, nurse, housemaid— the whole kit and caboodle. Don't ask me why." Mrs. Hildebrand looked placid; obviously, you should ask her why.

"Sounds very odd. To fire a whole household."

"She gave them all a decent severance pay. Two months, three months—I'm not exactly sure. I know this from my friend. Bella Merrick. Bella just happened to need a new cook, and when she called the Norris Agency, there was this woman available. You know Norris? They're the best."

Linda knew. It was where she had gotten Claudette.

"Bella said she didn't want anyone if there'd been trouble, but no trouble at all, Miss Norris told her. Just Mrs. Stanhope had decided to have a new staff for when her husband came home."

Suddenly Linda remembered something. *Someone made an overture to our receptionist.* Back to that. Oh, very much back to that. Suppose while Rosalie was working at New Beginnings, she had taken money from one of those avid couples and then failed to deliver on whatever it was she had promised. Suppose further that the couple, having missed the announcement of her marriage, had been looking ever since for that pretty receptionist—of course she couldn't risk having her picture in the paper. And suppose still further she was still up to those dirty dealings, and she wasn't sure what indiscreet conversation one of her domestic staff might have heard, and with her husband coming home, she felt it safer to get them all out.

Now it was Linda's turn to twirl her hands. She thought of all the wrong turns she had taken these last three days. She followed Maxine into a courthouse, and all she got for her efforts was a front-row seat at the scene of a mother's heartache. She sent Lenny chasing into a nightclub, and he came back with a story that was already known to the police. She had suspected these Hildebrands, and they turned out to be simply your standard scared and snobbish parents. Can she really go off on another tangent? Can she trust her own instinct?

Linda opened her top desk drawer. Four days ago, she'd put in there the picture of Elena she used to keep on her desk. Elena at three months snapped after her bath—just the bare shoulders and the proudly uplifted head.

"Listen. Could I talk to this woman? The new cook? What's her name? If you could ask your friend and arrange it for me, I'd be really grateful."

FIFTEEN

THE COOK'S NAME was Millie Brown, and half an hour later she was talking to Linda in the Merricks' den. Mrs. Hildebrand had arranged it. Called her friend, led the way in her car while Linda followed in hers, even suggested a coverup explanation: Just say you're writing an article; anyone gets flattered being pumped for something that will appear in print.

The den was different from the Hildebrand sunporch: dark leather furniture, rows of books, models of boats—this was a sailing family. The family was not in evidence; Linda's business was only with the cook. A stout woman, Millie Brown, with the settled kind of heaviness that looks as if it has been part of one forever. She had worked for the Stanhopes for ten months, was what she said. And she wished she could report on fancy dinner parties—that's what she expected when she saw that house. But the fact was, she did mostly the kind of plain cooking you don't need her talents for. When she came, Mrs. Stanhope was pregnant, a hard pregnancy, poor little thing, so they didn't go in for entertaining. And Dr. Stanhope leaving when the baby was six days old.

"Anyhow, it wasn't food he was interested in. It was that baby. He was wild for it—you can put that in your article. He'd make some excuse to go into the nursery ten times a day, Irma used to tell me. Oh. The nurse. And if the baby was outside, you can bet he'd be standing next to the carriage. Well, she is a picture, that child. Pretty as one. But you want to know about him. The cooking.''

Millie Brown tugged at her uniform. Not much cooking after he left, she has to admit. Mrs. Stanhope, she'd be out half the time. What's she saying! More than half. And if she was home, she didn't much care what she ate. Something light, Millie, she'd say. Not that she has to watch her figure, but it's those skinny ones that do the worrying. A little scallopini, maybe. A salad. Millie Brown's famous watercress soup that she's making for the Merricks tomorrow. And white wine to top it off. Yes. Mrs. Stanhope does go for her wine.

Linda looked out the window; gardeners were raking the leaves under a grove of birches. "Did she ever tell you she was dissatisfied?"

Dissatisfied! The settled face looked up.

"She did dismiss three of you."

"Don't ask me what that was all about."

"Just what I am asking."

Millie Brown sniffed. "Just two weeks ago she told me what we'd have to do to get ready for her husband. All the months he's up there, he eats this tinned stuff. Only thing you can get at that freezing place. So we had to fill him up on the fresh food he loves. Fresh fruit. Fresh vegetables. She was going to have some market in the city deliver, you can't count on stores around here." Dissatisfied: what was Linda talking about.

"You must have some idea why she let you go."

The woman leaned her arms on either side of the chair. "You know what I think. She panicked, poor little thing. What is she? Twenty-five years old? Twenty-six? And not too competent at running things, only don't put that in your article. And there's that husband everyone knows about. You should've heard the phone, weeks before he was due to come home. She told them all the same thing. I'm sorry, I can't help you. Can't help—it was the truth. She'd come into the kitchen, putter around, forget what she wanted to say, pour a glass of wine, go out. You know, flighty. So what does a flighty little woman do when she's scared. She just blindly hits out."

Flighty little woman—it was an accusation, but also an exculpation. It made Rosalie Stanhope helpless and endearing at the same time as she was frivolous and foolish. Linda kept her gaze on those gardeners outside. She might have known. You can't get a straight story from a participant. Surely not a participant with a need to guard her own pride. If a capable worker like Millie Brown has been fired from a job, she has to tamper with the episode. She has to make the woman who offended her the victim of her own fears and insecurities.

"Can you tell me what happened when she said she was letting you go?"

"What should happen. She told June and me together. June Cotts—she was the housemaid. She'd
told Irma the night before. She said we should pack
up, and we did, and I said I wanted to say good-bye to
Mara—that's the baby. Not that she would know the
difference, but that sweet thing, I couldn't bear to
leave without seeing her one more time. But Mrs.
Stanhope, she said the baby was sleeping, and besides, she'd ordered a taxi to take us to the station and
it was due any minute. And the taxi came and that was
it. The whole story."

Linda waited a minute, looking at the plaques,
banners, medals that commemorated races—the
Merricks were not just sailors, they were serious sailors. Finally she said if Millie Brown would call June
Cotts and Irma Lynch for her, if she would do that, it
would be a big help.

The woman pulled at her apron. June wouldn't have
any different story to tell. But if Miss Stewart wants to
take the time, fine with her. So wait here. Just take a
second.

Millie Brown was right. When Linda got there, it
appeared that June Cotts liked to talk, was glad to
talk, but for all the garrulous flow, she had little to
add. She worked in a house about eight miles distant,
a ranch-type model that was one of a cluster of three
on the edge of a golf course, and she was ironing. She
hoped Miss Stewart wouldn't mind. Her family was
away, and she wanted to get these curtains done before they returned. So now what was it? Something

about Dr. Stanhope, Millie had said. An article about him. She's not surprised. She knows how famous he is. Imagine, a man going to those freezing places and living in—is it huts?—and eating that food. Not so young either. Fifty-four. Fifty-four on his last birthday, she knows for a fact. And plenty of money. Rich! Wouldn't you think he'd want to stay home? Especially with that pretty wife and the baby. The baby he's wild about. When the baby was born, he gave them all champagne. Something Miss Stewart can write in her article. He came home from the hospital and he opened a bottle of champagne and had everyone in the house to drink it with him. Even the gardener. Even a man washing windows. I have a daughter, he kept saying. Me with a baby daughter.

"You have to excuse this room," June Cotts went on. "I'm supposed to iron in the kitchen, that room in there with the big windows. But it faces the golf course and I'm always scared a golf ball will come through. All those men hitting any which way, it might happen. A ball crashing through that window."

"I wonder if you ever heard Mrs. Stanhope conducting any kind of business," Linda said. "Any business deal at all."

The hand holding the iron slowed, but on the smooth face there was no sign of agitation. That pretty little thing doing business? She had enough with that house. Too much, all those rooms and the stairways and the gardens outside. "She could never do any business," June Cotts said. "She wasn't the type.

Even making a schedule was too much for her—half
the time she didn't know who was scheduled to do
what. She'd stand there, that glass of white wine in one
hand and a piece of paper in the other, and I'd feel
sorry for her. She did her best, but it was just too
much.''

June Cotts bent again; the curtain was flowing in a
white froth onto the floor. This house she's working
in now, that's something different. Four bedrooms,
three baths—you have things under control. If not for
those golf balls, she would be content. She can't figure it. All the beautiful land around here, why would
anyone build a house where a golf ball could kill you.
Well, you won't catch her ironing on that side, you
surely won't. Miss Stewart should watch it when she
goes out. Hasn't happened yet, but you never know.

A golf ball did not hit Linda, but lassitude did. Two
down, one to go, and so far not a single incriminating
fact—is there any reason for her to press on? However, she called Irma Lynch, who had not yet taken
another nursing job, who was in her own apartment,
and after a few minutes she got a grudging accep-
tance. All right, come then. Third house on the left,
second floor. Ring the bell.

She didn't have to ring. The address was a two-
family house with a trellis separating the two small
porches, and Irma Lynch was waiting on one of them.
With a mumbled word, she led Linda up a dim staircase. The living room on the second floor was also
dim, closed in with dark shades pulled severely down.

There were lamps on two small tables, but Irma Lynch didn't turn them on. She simply stood in the middle of the room and repeated what she'd said on the phone. She'd known Dr. Stanhope just six days. Not much you could learn about a man in six days. "He seemed nice enough," she said, "and he loved the child. What am I saying! He was mad for her. I'll never forget the scene when he had to leave. He'd made up this little song—bye-bye baby, see you soon. Not really a song, you might say a chant, and he stood there singing to her and crying at the same time. I saw it myself. This man carrying on because he had to part from his six-day-old child." Then she cut that off. That was it, she added briskly. All she knew. What else did Miss Stewart expect to hear?

Linda looked around. The room of a woman who spends most of her life in other people's houses. Lots of small knickknacks, placed with no special care on the shelves, a rug that was frayed around the edges, two faded watercolors. Plus a couch and two chairs where a guest might be asked to sit down. Linda was not asked to sit down. "Just seems so odd," she said tentatively.

"Odd?" The woman had graying hair that grew low on her forehead, an upright figure, a square noncommittal face.

"I've heard a little about what happened at the Stanhopes this week. Her asking a whole staff to leave at once."

Irma Lynch gave an airy wave. "Way it goes," she said.

"But didn't you feel terrible? After—how long was it? Almost a half a year. Just when you're used to a child, really attached to her, to have to quit?"

The woman shrugged. "Win some, lose some," she said.

"Well, did anything happen? You know," she pressed on, against the woman's unencouraging look—"some kind of trouble that would make a woman need to get rid of everyone."

"Trouble? Certainly not."

"Then what was her reason?"

"Whoever holds the money doesn't need a reason," Irma Lynch said with her implacable stoicism.

Linda sat uninvited in a chair. Win some, lose some; way it goes—there was something factitious about it. Practiced, fabricated. It was not what Claudette would have said. After taking care of a baby for five months, lowering her wrist to test the tepid bath, coaxing the nipple into the stubborn mouth, giving the persuasive pats to elicit the relieving burp—after all that, Claudette would not walk jauntily out. Win some, lose some?—not on your life. Claudette, that gentle, stalwart Claudette, would shout that she wanted an explanation. Don't think you can get away with this, Claudette would bluster. The agency will hear exactly what happened, Claudette would threaten. You'll never get anyone else to work for you, Claudette would confidently warn.

Irma Lynch was not so different from Claudette. The same patient face, tightly held bosom, hips broadened from all the sedentary hours. And also, surely, the same collection of exemplary references. So why this cavalier act? Why the flippant unconcern?

The woman walked over to the window. The shade was still down, but when she fiddled with it, light illumined her face. Linda stared. That wiry hair hanging low over her forehead, the erect stance, the offended gaze.

"Goodness. I just realized. Weren't you at that dinner?"

"Dinner?"

"For the Center. Last Tuesday. I'm a counselor there—I was at the table next to you."

As if recognizing the light as a danger, the woman stepped away from the window. She may have been at the dinner, she guardedly said. Hard to remember everything.

"You could hardly forget this. Mrs. Stanhope made a speech. You said she was a little tramp."

"Now I remember. I was tired. I sometimes say things when I'm tired."

She didn't look as if she could ever be tired. You could see her, getting up at midnight for an infant's peremptory wail, and again at two, and then indomitable, uncomplaining, walking the floor from four to five.

"You sounded as if you knew something. Something special,"-Linda said.

"Whatever I said, I take it back."

Linda had the same feeling she'd had when she first called: the woman was saying no, but she seemed not unwilling to go on saying it. She simply stood in the middle of her rug with her arms folded and her expression mildly taunting. Linda spoke slowly. "Actually, Rosalie Stanhope does seem to arouse complicated emotions in people."

It happened all at once. Like striking a match. The slow rage heating her, the color creeping from her neck up the affronted cheeks. Irma Lynch didn't raise her voice, which gave to the accusations an extra edge of venom. Rosalie Stanhope didn't deserve what she had. Not that beautiful house that could go to rack and ruin for all she'd lift a finger to take care of it. Not the husband who did all that great work only Rosalie couldn't care less. And not the baby. God knows not the baby. It was a sin, really. Such an uncaring mother. In just the six days he was home Dr. Stanhope came in to pick up the baby more than Rosalie did in the whole five months. "I want to say goodnight to her, don't forget," Rosalie would say. She was the one to forget. She'd be so busy trying on some new dress or admiring the new hairdo that when you brought the baby in she would hardly look up. "Cute," she would say. "Really cute." But it was herself she was looking at. Her reflection. That pretty head at her dressing table, surrounded by the jars and bottles. And the glass of white wine, be sure not to leave that out.

"Once the baby had a rash on its chest. It turned out to be nothing, just roseola after a fever, but she didn't even notice. 'I think we should call the doctor,' I said, and she couldn't figure out why. She never looked under the shirt. What am I saying. 'Doctor'! She took the baby once, but it turned out you had to wait your turn. Had to sit in the room with the other mothers. Boring, boring. So next month, for the regular checkup, she told me to do it. You don't believe me? Ask Doctor Sawicky. It's the one thing all mothers like to do—take the children for the checkups. A gain of nine ounces, the doctor says, and the mother beams, like its some great triumph of hers. Maybe it is some great triumph of hers. But not this mother. After I'd come back, she wouldn't even want the details. She'd ask, but not really. She didn't listen. Her mind wasn't on it."

The red blotch was gone from the heavy cheeks. This was what she'd been holding in under the pretense of jauntiness. Relief had superseded anger.

"Women like that, they're trash. They get it all, house and husband and baby. And they don't deserve any of it. They're useless. Worse than useless. They ruin things. Do damage. You think I'm awful, don't you, saying these things. Well, I've been around, I've seen plenty, I know about women like her."

Linda gave a neutral nod. How much of this kind of tirade could you believe? I've been around, I've seen plenty...that at least must be true. Irma Lynch might be fifty or fifty-five or sixty—the steely hair and spreading figure afforded no certain clues. But in any case, you knew there had been years and years when she was taken into the heart of families, lived with them on terms of intimacy, stayed for the two or three or perhaps four years until her particular ministrations were no longer needed, then left to start the process all over. Did that make her a reliable observer? Or did it breed the kind of bitterness that distorts vision, makes one unduly critical of whatever is frivolous and light-hearted and appealing in those she works for?

In a way, Linda thought, this woman's testimony about Rosalie Stanhope was as suspect as Mrs. Hildebrand's—the one stemming from grievance about her life, the other from snobbery about her territory.

"Her firing us all, that was typical," Irma Lynch said.

"How do you mean?"

"Did she think for a second of that baby? A five-month-old baby having to change nurses? Not her. That wouldn't cut any ice with Rosalie. It's herself she's worried about. Her safety."

"I don't get it."

"Why do you suppose she let everyone go?"

"I've been trying to figure it out."

"So we wouldn't tell her husband on her. She wouldn't take a chance of that. No. Couldn't."

Linda felt the excitement coursing under her skin. Now at last, at last! "Wouldn't tell him about what?"

"About the man she was seeing, of course."

Linda felt her shoulders slump.

"A little tramp like her, what other way do you think she'd cheat on her husband?"

"I don't know. I don't know."

"Did I ever get to see him? She's too smart for that. She never even let him come to the house. But I saw the way she dolled up before she went out. I saw her come back home at three A.M. Plenty of times when I was up with the baby I'd see her driving in must've been close to morning. Don't tell me she was at the movies till that hour." In the adjacent apartment, someone walked heavily down the stairs, but not a sound in this room where a woman's liturgical voice composed the annals of infidelity. "Now I think of it, once he was there. The night she fired me. At least I guess it was him."

Linda gave a listless nod, but Irma Lynch no longer needed encouragement to keep going. "What a way to do it. A nurse comes back from her Sunday off at ten o'clock, and that's when she gets the news. Pack up. Out. Finished."

"So you left the next morning?"

Irma Lynch turned in surprise. "Next morning? Right now, that was the ticket. She said a taxi would be coming, could I get ready in twenty minutes. I got ready in ten, then I went down the hall to kiss the baby one last time. But she said no. Be better if I didn't go in, she said, she didn't want a scene. A scene. Imagine her saying that. God, I hated her. I hated her so much I was willing to hurt myself just to get at her—

that's how I felt. I decided not to take her money, I was going to throw it back in her face. But I weakened. I'm ashamed to say I weakened. She held it out, a check for three months' salary, and I took it."

"You were right," Linda said. "That would've been crazy, to give it up."

"I guess I felt a little crazy then."

She didn't look crazy now. She shivered for a second, as if the recital of that night had touched something deep inside her, but she looked sober, thoughtful, staid.

"One more thing. How come you were at that dinner?"

"Oh, that. I knew about it, of course, we all did. Her planning to make the big speech instead of him. So I sat here brooding, and I got this idea. When she got up to talk, I'd expose her. Don't laugh. I'd stand up and say all the terrible things I knew about her. I even paid twenty-five dollars to get in—that's how important it was." Irma Lynch gave a smile—her first. "I didn't even eat. All that good food and I didn't touch a thing—I was saving myself for my big effort. I knew exactly what I would say. 'This woman, don't believe what she says about loving her own child. She doesn't even know what she weighs. Her own child, and she doesn't know what she weighs.' But when the time came, I didn't do a thing. You were there, you know I didn't. I looked around at all the those people dressed up in their best, and I sat there like a dummy."

A dummy muttering, Little tramp. "You did right," Linda said again.

The woman moaned, but her face was calm. "You think I'm making too much of it, don't you?"

"Well..."

"It's that baby, that's what it is. Losing a baby after you take care of it for five months, you can't imagine how it feels."

Going out the door, Linda said all the right things. Mean story... horrid... unspeakable... sorry. Everything except the salient fact that she did in fact know about the feelings attendant on that particular loss.

SIXTEEN

"YOU'RE A very persistent woman, Miss Stewart," Wilkerson said. She had come to his office after leaving Irma Lynch. He didn't pretend to be pleased to see her; in fact he said that in another five minutes he would have been gone, which sounded like another way of saying he wished he had been gone. But since he was here, he listened attentively while she told him about the three women who had worked for Rosalie Stanhope and under circumstances of some obscurity been fired. It was a long report, but he sat in silence. A silence that went on after her voice wound down, so she spoke with more irritability than she had intended.

"Don't you think there's something peculiar?"

It was surely peculiar, Wilkerson said, in that most people didn't have a domestic staff of three people to dismiss.

"I mean, of course, it's peculiar to fire them all at once."

Wilkerson picked up the phone, dialed a number, and told someone he'd be there in a few minutes. Then he gave his impassive nod. "Miss Stewart, have you ever met Rosalie Stanhope?"

"No."

"No contact with her whatsoever?"

"I heard her speak at our annual dinner this week."

"What I think is peculiar is that with no provocation at all you'd busy yourself with the domestic arrangements of a woman you don't know."

Linda sat on the edge of her chair. Her third visit to this office, and it had the same look of cluttered officialdom as the first time. Wrong: a change after all. The black letters on the pile of yellow *No Parking* signs signified Thursday instead of Saturday as the forbidden day. Also, a couple of new posters. Or at least a couple she had not noticed before. One announced a field day at a place called Camp Willow Pond. *Fun for All. All Welcome. Sunday, November 4.* One specified the hours on three different days when bicycle tests would be available. *Unless You Take the Test, You Cannot Get a License for Your Bike.* But nothing had been displaced to accommodate these new posters. *Field Day* was taped over a frayed *Most Wanted List. Bicycle Tests* hung so it almost but not quite concealed *Incest Hotline*. It was like Wilkerson himself. Welcome all view. Discard nothing. Treat every opinion with the same guarded neutrality.

"I do know something about Rosalie Stanhope," she said. "When she worked as a receptionist for the New Beginnings agency, someone made an overture to her. A couple who'd been turned down for getting a child by the accredited channels. In a job like that, she could have met up with lots of such couples. She would have their names."

"An overture. Do you know whether a bribe was actually passed?"

She had to admit she didn't.

"Miss Stewart, based on this kind of nonevidence, are you saying you suspect Mrs. Stanhope of engaging in illegal tactics to procure children for wealthy people?"

"It's possible. It's also possible that's why she fired those women. Irma Lynch thinks it was because she was carrying on with a man and she didn't want her husband to find out. Millie Brown and June Cotts think she was just overwhelmed. But suppose it was something else. Suppose she'd made some careless phone calls, or some messages came through, something that in future someone in the household might interpret as sounding damaging, and she just decided to play it safe."

More silence. Wilkerson put his hand on the phone, but not to call that waiting person. If there was a waiting person. Then he made the remark. "You're a very persistent woman, Miss Stewart."

Persistent. He meant stubborn. He meant troublesome, pushy, didactic, foolhardy. Then he pointed to one of the posters. "See that? No, not the bicycle tests, the one about a field day. Camp Willow Pond. How do you think policemen's children can afford a weekend at their own camp?"

"I didn't know it was your own."

"Ours for six weeks a year. The rest of the time the Boy Scouts or firemen or some other local groups use it. A place at the edge of the bay with marsh and woods around where kids can learn things they never get a chance at. Like cooking over a fire and sleeping out and exploring and getting on intimate terms with nature. I have two boys. Ten and twelve. To listen to them, the weekends at that camp are the best thing in their life."

"I don't get it."

"I thought you knew. Dr. Stanhope bought the tract and gave it to the county."

"I see."

"That's not all he's done. Last summer the son of one of our policemen was badly injured diving into a shallow pool. The boy should've known better, but he did it. Dr. Stanhope is paying for all the rehabilitation. Years and years it will be, at best he'll never walk."

"You mean, because Stanhope is so rich and generous, his wife doesn't need money? But what if she's planning to leave him? What if Irma Lynch is right, and the affair is a serious one?"

Wilkerson pointed out that they weren't in the business of checking out marital fidelity.

"So you're not going to do anything?"

"What would you have us do?"

"I still think if a woman does something so unusual as to fire three people for no reason, if there's even a slim chance that it's connected to a murder case."

"As far as I can see, the connection is all in your head. Like I said, you're a difficult woman, Miss Stewart." It was not what he had said. However, he leaned forward with the air of one making a concession. "Since you're so persistent, I'm going to tell you."

"Tell me what?"

"Why she fired those people. I didn't want to, but you give me no choice."

She stared at him. The second time he had done it: sat with his inexpressive face, while she, feeling a grim exaltation and speaking in laborious detail, divulged something of which he had been apprised all along.

"You understand, this is not to go further."

"For heaven's sake, just tell me."

He spoke with great deliberation. "As a matter of fact, Mrs. Stanhope had a kidnapping scare."

"Someone tried to take her child?"

"It didn't get that far. She found a scrap of paper. Part of a letter someone had evidently thought they were throwing away and failed to completely dispose of. It said—wait, I have it. Filed under Tuesday, October twenty-second, which is when she came. Here. '...have B on south lawn behind rose trellis between 11 and 12. We can have 3—'"

"Three what?"

"We don't know. That's all there is. Cars? Men? Anyone's guess."

"Where did she find this?"

"I believe she said a kitchen wastebasket. She's a heavy smoker, though she knows she shouldn't be. As she tells it, she was bending down to throw away an empty pack, and she saw this scrap of paper, and out of curiosity she picked it up.''

''B. . . it could be anything.''

''A panicked mother with a five-month-old infant who is taken for an airing on the south lawn of her house every morning would naturally think it meant baby.''

''Did she panic?''

''How else would she react? A woman with no one to turn to, her husband out of reach. She sat here trembling, poor brave little woman, trying not to cry.''

For a second Linda thought of all the different ways in which people had referred to Rosalie Stanhope. Our pretty Rosie: Lee Hevessy. Flighty little woman: Millie Brown. Little piece of fluff: Sally Hildebrand. Lying no-good tramp: Irma Lynch. Rich bitch: aspiring photographer. Even the varied responses she herself had felt: envious resentment at the dinner, plus, from time to time, those vagrant jolts of sympathy. And now here is Wilkerson: poor brave little woman. The curly hair, the cupcake face, the whole aspect of threatened motherhood, even the inability to give up smoking—right to his vulnerable heart.

''Did she tell you she was going to fire her whole staff?''

''It's one reason she came—to get my opinion. She hated to do it. The innocent along with the possibly guilty. But she said she couldn't function with the thought that someone in her own household, someone she saw every day, might be ready to betray her. I said I could certainly understand her feelings."

"Did she ask for police protection?"

"I told her we'd keep watch, of course. But that estate—what is it? Twenty-some acres? Take a lot of men to patrol an area that size. Besides, she had already hired detectives herself. Very sensible, I told her."

He put the papers about the Stanhope case back in a file. Then he said he understood how distressed she was, it was only natural. But these things took time. They were working on it; she must believe they were working on it. No, they still had nothing definite, no clues to the murder of that unfortunate Jenna Walsh either. He appreciated her having come in, but now he advised her to go home and rest. Friday night. She should have a restful weekend, and perhaps by next week progress would be made.

He sounded like Fran, though without Fran's large portion of sweetness and caring. She did go home, but she did not have a restful night, and next morning she called Lee Hevessy at home.

"Linda? Oh, Linda Stewart. Of course I remember."

"I wanted to ask you about Rosalie Stanhope. An overture, you said. An overture from a frustrated couple. So I wondered..."

In the instant before Lee answered, she heard Wilkerson: What I think is peculiar is that with no provocation at all you'd busy yourself with the domestic arrangements of a woman you don't know. She couldn't explain it to him then, she can't explain it to herself now. All she knows is she is obsessed by this woman, compelled by the ambiguities.

"How about eleven o'clock Monday?" Lee was saying. "No, let's say lunch. Linda, I can meet you for lunch on Monday."

She folded the local newspaper. On page 2 was the article about Claude Stanhope. *Noted Scientist and Explorer Returns after Arctic Ordeal.* And above it a picture not of Rosalie but of him. Thin gray hair, sunken cheeks, small mouth—all redeemed, or almost redeemed, by eyes with their look of quiet authority. Runty-looking? Not really.

"Monday will be too late," she heard herself say. "I have to—"

"Linda, I'm leaving here in two minutes. It's my one morning to play tennis. I have a date with Angie Hoffstra at nine."

"Where's your court?"

"Summit Park. The only public courts around. You sign a week in advance, and if you're even a minute late—"

"I'll meet you there. Lee, please. It won't take more than five minutes, I promise. I just have to talk to you."

Lee didn't say anything before she hung up. Did that mean she wouldn't talk? She wouldn't acknowledge Linda? She was there, at any rate, a gangly figure in a white skirt, white jacket, standing on the path that led

to the courts. And when Linda approached, she was
not pleased. Not even a half-hearted show of pleasure. Angie wasn't here yet, but look for her any second. Angie has never been late, not in all the years
they've been playing together. Quarter to nine now—
at nine sharp, the court is theirs. They have to get right
on, otherwise Angie will never forgive her. After all,
at ten o'clock someone will be waiting to throw them
off. Linda doesn't understand the pressure. Different
for those rich people around here who have their own
courts, can saunter on and off all day. But when you
have exactly sixty minutes, when that's it for the week.

Linda waited through this stormy monologue. That
resentment of rich people—if you worked in a suburb
like this, maybe you could never escape it. You felt it
even if you didn't articulate it as Lee Hevessy contin-
ually did. "Lee, can we sit over there?"

"I won't be able to see Angie if we're sitting down."

For a few years after she graduated from college,
Linda had played tennis. It was in a medium-size city
where the insufficiency of courts was a subject for
constant letters in the local paper. Now as she watched
the tense expression of the players waiting to get on,
it all came back. The suspense about the weather. The
tyranny of the clock. The feeling of never getting quite
enough. The desperate need to utilize every minute.

"Lee, that business about an overture. What did
you mean?"

"I'm sorry I said it. It was nothing. I don't want to
get anyone in trouble."

Next to them, two men were having an argument. I bought the balls last time. No, me, I remember distinctly. No, I did, it was right on this spot that... "I'm the one in trouble," Linda said.

Lee looked up at the sky, where a dark cloud was looming from the north. "It better not rain before we have our hour," she said.

"What about that overture?"

Lee pointedly took her racket out of the case, as if this would prove something to Linda. "Just because someone saw them together. Rosie and this couple. Mr. and Mrs. X—I don't want to mention their name. A scene in a restaurant—that's all there was to it."

"You must have meant something. Two days ago you said—"

"There's Angie. Angie! Over here."

Angie swung her racket as she walked down the slope from the parking lot. And she responded with the most perfunctory of nods to the introduction to Linda: a woman not even in tennis clothes. They were on number six, she told Lee. She just hoped that the beginners' doubles game wasn't next to them like last time.

"That was impossible. We spent half the time getting their balls."

"I'm going to check the names. If it's that same group—Lee, I'll meet you on the court."

A reprieve. They had five minutes. "What about that couple?"

"Just that we'd turned them down. I forget. Something about their not having a settled home, traveling all the time. Very wealthy, but for business reasons they had to travel. And then someone saw them at a restaurant with Rosie. The Pine Hollow Inn—an out-of-the-way place in Plummers Bay. Linda, that's the whole thing."

It can't be the whole thing. "Your court isn't ready, it's not nine."

"Sometimes the eight o'clock people get off early."

"Lee, listen. Rosie and this couple. Did that someone see them passing money? An envelope with money—was that it?"

"Nothing like that." But something made Lee relent—was it the dismay on Linda's face? a nudge from her own conscience?—and as if she had not already turned down the bench, she grabbed Linda's arm and led her over there. "I don't want anyone to hear. Linda, this can't go any further. But what happened"—the deep voice dropped to a whisper—"what happened was that a few days later, a pregnant girl we'd been working with called up that she'd changed her mind. Her name was Gloria. She said she wouldn't give us the baby. Not us, of course; some couple named Millhouse were in line to get it. She was due in about two months; it had all been settled. We thought it was all settled. But now out of the blue, Gloria changed her mind."

"You think it was not out of the blue at all?" Though none of the waiting players was within earshot, though no one evinced any interest in the two women leaning together on a bench, she lowered her voice to match Lee's. "You think Rosalie told that couple about Gloria, and they approached her with an offer? A good offer? More, anyhow, than she could get under your legal auspices?"

Lee pushed at a loose edge of tape around the handle of her racket. She took a ball out of the can and put it back in. Then she said it was possible. Barely possible. Now, really, she had to go.

"Lee, wait a minute. What happened to the girl? Gloria. What made you think—"

"She moved to another state to have the baby. Maine. That's what her family told us when we called. And the couple also went up there. They had a house—an island, really—off the Maine coast. Linda, it's all speculation. Not a shred of real evidence. And the Millhouses didn't suffer. They went to the top of our list, six months later they—"

It was not the Millhouses she cared about.

"Angie's waving. That means the people are getting off."

"Just a second. Did you ever accuse Rosalie? Say anything to her?"

Lee stood up, she resumed her normal, resonant voice. "Why should we? Right after that was when Claude Stanhope spotted her. It went very fast, that wild courtship. That famous middle-aged man, our pretty scatter-brained receptionist—we were all stunned. Just two weeks later she came and told us she was getting married.''

"So you didn't pursue it? Do any investigation?''

The path was crowded—people coming up from the courts, people going down to the courts. I told you that net game would do it, a girl shouted to her partner. "Investigate? How do you investigate? Where do you start? We're an adoption agency. We're overworked as is. We can't go in for investigations.'' Then that softening came over her. "I explained, Linda. It's such a tiny percentage, that dirty dealing. If there really is any dirty dealing. Besides''—Lee gave a little skip, walking fast down the gravel path—"it was over. No hard feelings. The secretaries even gave Rosie a send-off. Champagne and cheese, the last afternoon she was there. We all came. Everyone was happy. Well, I guess Jay wasn't happy, but that's life.''

"Jay?'' Linda was running to keep up.

"The boyfriend. Linda, I really can't—''

"Lee!'' She grabbed hold of the white jacket. "That Jay, what was his last name?''

"God, I don't remember.''

"Was it Earling?''

Angie had stationed herself on the far side of the court, she was performing practice serves. "Lee, was it?''

"Could be. Earling—that sounds familiar. Cute fellow, I told you. We called him Boy Scout. Rosalie, Boy Scout is waiting for you.''

Yes. The boyish forelock, the eager gaze, the bullying conviviality: Boy Scout to a T. "Lee, one more thing. Has Rosalie ever come back? I mean, does she have any contacts now so she could still—"

"Oh, Linda, I can't talk. Angie would kill me. Christ, I didn't mean to say that. But Angie's waiting, I really do have to run."

She ran fast. When Linda looked back from the top of the hill, they were batting a ball back and forth, two women who felt the desperate need to utilize every minute.

SEVENTEEN

IRMA LYNCH was grudging but polite. Okay, come if you have to, she said on the phone. When Linda got there, she was again led upstairs, into the living room that did not produce an invitation to sit down. This time, however, the shade was halfway up, you could see the knickknacks on the shelves. Two ceramic deer, a painted candelabra, decorated plates, a birchbark canoe, another candelabra, mugs with writing in Arabic: bits and pieces carved out of other people's vacations. We brought you this little remembrance, the donors would have said, handing over a pine cushion to commemorate the mountain they had climbed, a pair of wooden bears from their Scandinavian sojourn. Did Linda forget anything, was her greeting.

"I wanted to ask you more about Mrs. Stanhope."

"I thought it was him you were writing about."

That fabricated excuse from a day ago—it had slipped her mind. She said Dr. Stanhope, yes, sure. But his wife was also important.

However, a curtain had come down. Irma Lynch folded her arms and said Mrs. Stanhope was not half bad. Not when you compared. She never went poking into your dresser drawers, like some employers did when the nurse had her day off. She never counted what was in the fridge to see did you eat too much fruit or finish off that leftover chicken. She never went through the baby's clothes, did you maybe make off with a little sweater for some child you knew at home. Miss Stewart would be surprised. She'd been in plenty of houses where the madame did just that. All the money in the world, and that was the kind of niggardly housekeeping that went on. You had to balance everything. Being left alone—that was a big blessing.

Linda looked out the window. The sun was out, any trace of black cloud gone. A bonanza for Lee and Angie—at least they'd be able to finish their hour. "I didn't mean to offend anyone. I'm sure it was a fine house to work in."

"I'll be lucky if I get a place as good the next time."

So that was it. Irma Lynch was worried about her next job. She envisaged a network that passed comments, relayed secrets, made judgments; and in some vigilant corner of her mind, she had allocated Linda to this prejudicial system.

"I would never dream of repeating anything you said."

"I have to get a job soon. I've been holding off—some people can do that. They have resources. They can afford to take it easy. But if you work as a baby nurse, you better keep working if you want to eat." That glum distaste for anyone a step ahead on the ladder—she sounded like Lee Hevessy.

"Believe me, whatever you said is safe with me."

"I didn't say anything." Irma Lynch took her stoic stand next to the cluttered shelf. Tramp...careless...useless...damage: in the interest of expediency, all wiped out.

Linda said what she was interested in, actually, was the man Irma Lynch had mentioned. The one she thought Rosalie Stanhope used to meet night after night. Did the nurse ever get a glimpse of him?

"I told you. She was too smart."

"How about on the phone? Did she mention his name? She might have said, oh, I'll be there at eight o'clock, and then maybe a name?"

Not that either.

When Linda paused for breath, it occurred to her that this could be the end of the road. She had studiously followed every lead, tracked down in its circuitous bypath every clue. She now knew that Rosalie Stanhope, whose husband supported the Center, and Jay Earling, who did legal work for the Center, had been a pair, a serious pair, before Rosalie's marriage. But where did that lead? What did it signify? If this interview proved a washout, she was finished.

"What happened that one time you say he came to the house?"

"What time?"

"The night she fired you."

"I'm not even sure who it was. I heard two people in her room, but the door was closed."

"What'd they say? What?"

"I don't remember. I wasn't listening. I told you—
I was ordered to get out. Like I was a thief, hustled out
in the middle of the night."

It's important, Linda wanted to say. It's of the ut-
most importance that you remember. But it was not
important for Irma Lynch. The only thing to which
she could attach importance was the indignity she had
suffered, the undeserved humiliation. A responsible
and devoted baby nurse for no reason given the boot—
why should she remember anything else?

Linda's hand went out absently, she fingered one of
the wooden bears. Once in a psychology course she
was taking, a doctor who practiced hypnotism came
to lecture. We don't pretend to be a substitute for long-
term therapy, he had said. But in certain areas, when
a patient wants to dredge something up from memory, or get over an irrational fear, or fight off a distasteful habit, we can chalk up authentic successes.
And don't believe the sensational stories you hear. We
don't go in for tricks. In hypnosis as performed by a
certified professional, our preferred setting is a dark-
ened room and the most exotic prop we use is a plain
round pocket watch that in certain circumstances we
dangle back and forth. And our only patter is a request for quiet, for total relaxation. But there is one
imperative. An indispensable requisite. The subject
has to truly want to accomplish the given result. If he,
or let's say she, says that stopping smoking is the reason for her visit, she has to have a real desire to stop
smoking. It doesn't matter if this desire comes from ill

health, or fear of future health, or simply the fact that her husband can't stand dirty ashtrays—the desire has to be genuine.

How could she make Irma Lynch want to dredge up a particular conversation? Suppose she told the truth: a murder…in fact, three murders…a tragic loss…a shady enterprise: would any of that penetrate the egocentric sense of injury in which the woman was encased?

Linda rubbed her tongue over her dry lips. "I wonder if I could have a glass of water."

It roused her hostess to minimal hospitality. She'd made coffee that morning, take a second to heat it up. If Miss Stewart would like that.

Linda waited in the living room—she was pointedly not asked to come inside—and when the coffee came it was good and strong. She drank half a cup before she spoke again.

"I've been thinking about that night. What Mrs. Stanhope did, firing you and the others, was really nasty. But did you ever think that it could also be illegal?"

"I don't understand."

"I know she gave you a generous amount of severance pay. But she made a commitment when she hired you. You especially. Taking care of a new baby—I'm sure she led you to understand the job would go on for at least a year. Of course if there had been any complaints, any cause for dissatisfaction."

Irma Lynch drew herself up. Dissatisfaction! What an idea!

"Exactly. So in a sense she broke a contract. Not a written one, obviously, but in some cases an oral one can signify as well."

"You mean we might be entitled to more than we got?"

"Just what I'm telling you. About the mechanism for you to get the recompense you deserve."

"Then there's some agency that might help us?"

Linda held her breath. The woman was nodding, going over it—believing it. Why shouldn't she? Illegal to break an oral contract with a domestic worker—it was not true, but to an inflamed mind, it might sound true. For a government agency to take action in this kind of grievance—it was not the way things worked, but in a reasonable world it was the way they should work. The premise of a retributive justice had struck a responsive chord.

"She shouldn't get off so easy," Irma Lynch said. "A couple of months' salary—what's that to her?"

Linda waited a second. Then she said if they were thinking about future action, they should first go over in detail everything that happened that night.

"She didn't find fault with a single one of us. Not one. She never mentioned anything we were doing wrong." It was still what seemed most compelling.

"That does put her in a weak position," Linda murmured. Another expectant pause. Then—"Maybe she voiced some complaint to that friend. The one who was in her room.''

''Oh, no. He was the one doing the talking.''

She watched Irma Lynch shake her head, as if to erase from it all irrelevancies. If I had a pocket watch, I could dangle it, she thought. ''Well, let's go back to it,'' she said quietly—at the same time, her hand went out to pull down the shade. ''It's late at night. You're tired—you're just in from your day off, and you've been told to pack your clothes. You're angry. You don't know what this ridiculous business is all about. You walk along the hall carrying a suitcase. You hear Mrs. Stanhope and a man talking.''

'''Of course I can pull it off, Rosie,''' Irma Lynch suddenly said.

''Pull what off?'' Linda whispered, but Irma Lynch was going on.

''It was the little suitcase I was carrying. I'd already taken the big one; I left it downstairs in the hall. Then I came back for my hat and coat and the little things. You know, the comb and brush and umbrella and stuff. I put on my hat, but I had my coat over my arm. I stopped for a minute at the door to her room. Now why did I do that?'' A pause, then a shrug. ''Yes. I thought I'd knock and she'd open it and say something else. Or I'd have a chance to ask a question. But the two of them went on talking. He said, 'Of course I can pull it of, Rosie. Don't forget I was once an actor.' Then he did that funny thing.''

Don't breathe. ''Funny how?''

"Talking like a woman. This high voice, like a woman. A woman with a sort of hoarse, scratchy voice. 'Now is the time for all good men to come to the aid of their country.' That's what he said in that scratchy woman's voice. Then in his regular voice he said, 'That's not my only trick.'"

My God! "Then what?"

"She giggled. I heard her giggling. 'Jay, you're a riot,' she said. I was furious, the idea of making jokes at a time like that, so I didn't knock on the door after all. I took my suitcase and went on."

Linda was furious too. The fury washed over her, leaving her weak, chilled; she had trouble making it down the stairs and into her car. Then she sat, while the sun the tennis players prayed for shone on the faded stoop, the two small porches, the upstairs window where a shade was an inch or two lower than when she'd come, and the fury gradually abated, it changed to something cold-blooded, thoughtful. She rolled down the window, and as she sat gripping the wheel, she thought that she might well do what she had conned Irma Lynch into doing. Turn back the clock. Relive some significant moments. Delve into memory.

It was people her imagination presented to her first. People she knew because of the tragedy, or knew better because of the tragedy than she had before, or knew without having met them at all. Marylou. Marylou's father. Maxine Hammond. Jay Earling. Jenna Walsh. Rosalie Stanhope. Even Claude Stanhope, who was visible only as a picture in a newspaper—even that man with his sunken face and high enterprise was real to her.

She also saw herself. As if she were simply another figure in the album, she saw a woman who had been obsessed with the idea of an illegal market in babies. It had been her dear conviction, her article of faith that she brooded about every day and carried staunchly through three scorching interviews with the police. During this week, she had visualized its machinations as one visualizes the icons of a religious belief. She saw the piles of cash changing hands, she imagined the furtive phone calls, she pictured the babies, those small sweet bundles, delivered at the covetous doors. She even composed, with involuntary sympathy, the rationale of the adoptive parents. In their own eyes, they had a moral justification. They might tread an illicit path, but they saw themselves as cherishing worthy aims.

But now, primed with a few facts she'd picked up in the last two days, this obsessed woman allowed herself to think along different lines. About that union between two attractive people that a stately marriage for one of them had not interfered with. About a photographer who had been prevented from taking a picture. About some women, innocent domestics, who had not been allowed a farewell kiss to a child. And about some discrepancies that existed when you put together the stories told by these women and by Lieutenant Wilkerson in his office.

Really wild discrepancies. Oh, Lieutenant Wilkerson, what about that thirty-six hour lag in the times! What about simple arithmetic!

But when she drove to the nearest phone booth and called him, he wasn't there. No, gone for the day. Sorry, Miss. If you'd like to speak to someone else.

She did speak to someone else. She hung up and called Lenny.

EIGHTEEN

"SAY THAT AGAIN," Lenny's groggy voice said; plainly, the phone had woken him.

"Lenny, you heard. A nurse's uniform. Your father once told me his nurse gets them from the laundry five at a time, so there must be one in the office. And she's just about my size."

"Can't you—"

"Buy one?" Once more at an outdoor phone booth; she saw a woman approaching with the look of uplifted resolve that meant she would expect her rightful turn at the instrument. "I looked up the only store that sells uniforms. It's in Plains and they're open Monday to Friday, and besides, I don't have time to drive to Plains." And when his answer was a muffled groan—"Lenny, you have a key to your father's office, don't you? I mean, it must be someplace round."

"You really want a *nurse's* uniform?"

"Oh my God. What do I have to—"

"Hey, I'm coming. I'm awake now, I'll get it."

She gripped the receiver. She'd forgotten: half past ten, of course he would be asleep. Eighteen-year-olds stayed up all night and slept all day. Even if they had nothing whatever to stay up for, they stayed. A debased routine from which they emerged at five in the

afternoon rosy, energetic, even-tempered, healthy.
"Also, a small medical kit," she said. "Never mind
what's in it. Just so it looks official."

"Linda. Is this more of—you know—"

"Yes. No. It's different. More important. Listen.
I'm in downtown Mayhew now, we have to get to
Mayhew Gardens. What's the best place for us to
meet?"

He was not just awake, he was functioning. "How
about Linden and Strand," he said. "That corner next
to the high school athletic field. I'll be there first."

He wasn't. She pulled over under the arching trees,
laid her head briefly on her arms, and then raised it to
watch the figures in the muddy field. A pick-up game
was in progress, with much fumbling of balls, ran-
dom running, shouted imprecations. And at the side,
a line of girls, the football groupies, in their bulky
sweaters and skintight jeans. She liked watching
them—the blowing hair, the distinctly outlined be-
hinds, the pert gestures of accessibility—but when two
of them detached themselves from the line and walked
in the direction of the car, she ducked her head. They
might know her. The girl on the left looked familiar;
she might be a client who had been at the Center last
week, and she would wave and say, Hi, Miss Stewart,
maybe she would even stop to talk.

And Miss Stewart is exactly who, at this moment,
she can't afford to be. She has to divest herself of the
appurtenances of that woman in order to prepare
herself for her new persona. A nurse. A nurse who

works in a pediatrician's office. If the deception is to be convincing to a stranger, she first has to convince herself, she has to identify with this problematic woman as actors are said to identify with the characters whose roles they take on. What about this nurse, that's what matters now. Does she at heart dislike all those squalling children it's her job to mollify? Is she secretly in love with the doctor? After office hours, do the two of them make love on the stained couch in the waiting room, where the toys still lie scattered on the floor and the illustrations from children's books look down on them from the wall?

"Miss Stewart? Linda?" Lenny was at the car.

"Did you bring it?"

Of course he had brought it: the uniform in a bag, the kit dangling from his hand.

She thanked him; she said he'd been great. But though, handing over the items, he wore his usual look of exalted complicity, she had to erect barriers with him too. If she must not be Linda Stewart, he could not be Harold's son. Rather, he must slip into the role of anonymous driver, part-time helper, someone with whom she had only the merest connection. She said they would take his car because it was more impressive, and she would change in the back while he was driving, and she told him where they were going; but that was all she said.

It was enough. With his alert sympathy, his self-conscious zeal, he appropriated her detachment. He didn't ask for details. His straight back said if she wanted to keep the game plan to herself, that was all right with him. So there was silence as they drove along the curving roads where only an occasional signpost or the glimpse of a distant roof signified that somewhere behind the rolling lawns and banks of contrived shrubbery there might be a house. For her part, she didn't look at the scenery. She didn't care to get caught up in its extravagant lushness. She simply stared ahead, so her only view was the tufts of hair that grew too long on Lenny's young neck. But after he turned in at the designated driveway and drove on the road that led past unmowed fields on one side and a small pond on the other, she leaned forward. "Lenny, listen. I have to see that baby. The one who's here, in the house. That's all I want—just a look. I have a wild idea, it's so wild I don't dare to even talk about it. Oh. And my name. It's—let's see—Holly Brandt."

There were two cars parked in front of the house— Lenny stopped behind them. She stepped out gingerly, a woman wearing an unaccustomed white uniform and prepared to be accosted before she got to the door. Mrs. Stanhope had hired her own detectives, Wilkerson had said; she envisioned someone thin, moody, forceful emerging with practiced suddenness from between the rhododendron bushes. But no one stopped her as she climbed the stone steps and walked across the terrace that stretched along the front of the house, and she rang the bell. "Yes?" It was a butler in a correct dark uniform.

"I'm Dr. Sawicky's nurse. I've come about the test for the baby."

"What's that?"

Linda looked down at a piece of paper. "Mara Stanhope, that's the baby's name, isn't it?"

"Yes, but..." The man looked puzzled. Not alarmed or hostile or wary. Just puzzled. Maybe she'd better talk to Mrs. Stanhope, he said as he let her in.

But as she stood in the large front hall, it was Dr. Stanhope who emerged from a room on the left. She knew him right away. He was wearing a crewneck sweater and gray pants, and when he paused in the doorway, she thought she could credit the description of him. With his short stature, dark beard, receding hairline, slightly hunched-over back, he was undeniably runty. At the same time, the eyes that looked out from under heavy brows were kindly, attentive, thoughtful, and when he spoke, in a resonant voice, she understood how you could listen to him lecture, and be tricked into thinking you had a grip on some obscure subject and not realize until it was over that nothing had come through.

He asked what seemed to be the problem.

The butler coughed. It was something about the baby.

Linda turned. "I have it written down here. A check-up after ten days of that little condition after the DPT immunization. It's ten days today."

"What little condition?"

"It's probably nothing serious. But you know Dr. Sawicky. He just wants to be on the safe side."

"Maybe I'd better call my wife." With which he turned to the butler. Would he ask Mrs. Stanhope to come down for a minute?

She thought they would wait in silence; she was prepared to keep her attention on the massive chairs that lined the walls. But he walked over a few steps and said companionably that he'd just come home after a long absence; this was why he wasn't up to date on anything connected with his child.

Just a few words, but such tenderness, she thought, pronouncing the words "his child," and also such modesty—did he really suppose that anyone who came to this house would not have kept track of the travels of the celebrated Dr. Stanhope? She was going to say this. Then she decided that the less she said, the better. Instead, she let her gaze wander around the large hall, and she saw the suitcases. Six or seven of them lined up along one wall. Odd, in this kind of household, for suitcases still to be sitting in a front hall hours after a man's arrival.

"She'll be down in a second—ah, here she is now. Rosie, dear, this is a nurse from Dr. Sawicky's office, she says the baby is due for a test. Maybe you'll understand."

She didn't understand anything, Rosalie said, and her pouty little smile made of not understanding a merit.

"You know, Dr. Sawicky found a possibility of a slight reaction from the DPT immunization at the last visit. He said it might well be nothing, but he also said we should check again in ten days. It's exactly ten days today. But since there was some reluctance about having the baby come to the office on a weekend, he agreed that I might come to you."

"Rosie, you must remember."

She had been standing, one arm on the banister, on the third step. But now she came all the way down. She had on a cream-colored wool dress with tan leather trim around its collar and cuffs—above it the dark hair glistened in the hall's low light. She turned briefly to Linda—that offhand glance again. Then she said, "I didn't take Mara for her checkup ten days ago."

"But this woman says—"

"Oh, the baby was there, all right. I had a headache. The nurse took her."

"Then that's all right, Rosie dear. Let's call the nurse down, she'll surely—"

"A different nurse."

"Different?"

Rosalie Stanhope closed her eyes for a second. Only a second. "I had to change the nurse—Claude, I told you."

"Ah, yes. I'd forgotten." A spasm of pain crossed his face—for that instant, he looked like an old man. "Well, won't take a minute for Miss . . . ah . . ."

"Brandt," Linda said.

"For Miss Brandt to go up and check on whatever that small condition is."

"Mara's sleeping—you know how important that is. She was restless all morning—it took hours to get her down."

Linda said she would try to be very quick.

"I don't trust Dr. Sawicky." Rosalie spoke with a burst that suddenly energized her, drove the look of offended languor from her face.

"Rosie, what do you mean?"

"I was talking to Helen Ray. You know, Bert's wife. She goes to him too. He's an alarmist, we both agreed. He sees trouble when there's nothing at all. I'm going to switch doctors when we come back."

When we come back: Linda looked again across the hall. Of course. That set of matched luggage—the vanity case, the round case for hats, the clothing bags—not in the least what a man brings back from an expedition. They're pulling out, all of them. They're taking the child where she can't be reached.

"By all means, switch if you think best. But in the meantime we shouldn't take any risk."

"There'll be a doctor over there," Rosalie said. "A wonderful one—the hotel checked it out. If there's anything wrong, he'll be able to find it."

"Rosie dear, of course a fine doctor, excellent facilities." Again the voice with which he would win over an audience. Patient, tutorial, edifying. "However, if the pediatrician who's been seeing Mara since she's an hour old, if he finds something to be concerned about..."

"Another thing bout that Dr. Sawicky. He has a rough touch with the babies." The little quiver of Rosalie's shoulders suggested that the rough touch had impinged on them. "You should see how he handles them—no wonder there's all that screaming. A doctor like that, who doesn't even know how to handle babies."

"Rosie, we did a lot of checking before we decided to use Ralph Sawicky. He came with first-rate credentials. So if he says there's something that needs attention..."

"I'll be very quick," Linda said. "You can come up with me."

It was a mistaken tactic—she realized right away. She should have left it all to him: the mediating, the reasonableness, the supple attentions to his wife. She threw him off stride, so he shifted from defense to interrogation. This slight reaction, he said. She hadn't specified how it worked.

One of her fears, as she'd sat in the car planning this, was that with his scientific background, his fund of knowledge, Claude Stanhope would see right through her puny lies. Little reaction . . . to his trained ear, it would ring false. Now she realized that his ear was no more trained at recognizing childhood disorders than would be that of a lawyer, a banker. In fact, his concern for his daughter was so great, it swept away even the normal skepticism, the ordinary sense of wariness.

"In rare cases, it can develop into a muscular impairment," she said.

"For something that potentially serious, I think we would talk to the doctor himself," Claude Stanhope mildly said.

"Of course he's planning to talk to you. He's at a medical convention this weekend—he explained that at the last visit. But he also went into a very detailed explanation—that's his procedure—when the baby was four months old and he saw the preliminary signs."

"Rosie, you didn't write me there was trouble."

"No real trouble. I told you the baby was fine." She was back at the staircase, that artful position, one foot in its tan pump just lifted to the bottom step.

"Well, do you remember what he said?"

"Oh, Claude, it was that nurse who took her."

"For the four-month checkup too?" A faint scruple twisted the network of lines around his eyes. "Rosie, did you never go yourself?"

"I went the first time—I told you. It was horrid. This cramped waiting room, not even place for everyone, and a sick child drooling all over toys everyone else would handle, and the crying. When we come back, a pediatrician who knows how to run things." She tripped over next to her husband, she rested a hand lightly on his shoulder.

Her touch accomplished what it was meant to. Claude Stanhope cleared his throat. "Could you tell us exactly what you're looking for?" Linda on the stand again.

"It's called the Grolier syndrome, after a Dr. Leon Grolier of Boston who discovered it. A slight sensitivity in, as I said, a very small percentage of babies that causes a reaction to the immunization. The doctors notes it and checks after ten days."

"Checks how?"

To calm herself, she glanced over at the suitcases once more. Behind the vanity case, she saw the adjustable seat in which a baby can be supported while sitting up. The one she herself had used had been borrowed from people on the floor below, and the first time she put Elena in it, the spokes weren't properly adjusted so the whole contraption collapsed. Bending over the shrieking child, her heart stopped. Concussion. Brain damage. Broken spine. But thirty seconds later the usual beautific smile washed over the baby's face, and she realized what the doctor said was true: they're tougher than you think.

She patted the medical kit. "Simple. Just a matter of holding a flashlight to ascertain whether there's an imbalance in the dilation of the pupils when you exert pressure on the bent knee."

"Suppose you do find this imbalance." Dr. Stanhope seemed more stooped over, but his voice was steady: the judicious examiner.

"Then the doctor treats it so long as he gets it on time."

"How long a period qualifies for 'on time'?"

You couldn't be wholly alarmist; it was as likely to reduce credibility as to impel action. She said there was no emergency. The specific serum to combat the condition had to be administered within a week.

"A week." Rosalie put her hand to her hair: her signal of assertion. "The doctor in France can handle the whole thing. That's better anyhow. This business of a nurse, someone without a medical degree, making important decisions about my baby. And if the doctor over there doesn't have this...this serum, we'll have a messenger bring it."

Someone without a medical degree: it was a shrewd tack. For whatever reason Rosalie had made it, it was shrewd. She had failed in her attempt to undermine Dr. Sawicky, so she shifted to his surrogate, and it did the trick. It tipped the balance. It put this whole problematic procedure once more in the wrong. Rosalie Stanhope looked at Linda—that speculative glance again. Here in her own home, with her own husband, she was in charge, with new reserves of confidence or audacity. "So we thank you so much," she said, "and now that we know about the problem, we'll get in touch with Dr. Sawicky first thing Monday morning."

That drawling voice held the assurance of victory, and Dr. Stanhope confirmed it. Still mediating, he gave Linda his nicely apologetic smile. Then he said they were leaving on an arduous trip within an hour, and Miss Brandt could understand that they had a lot to do.

An hour. His deep voice tolled it out. He knew about Rosalie's negligence, her indifference, her little fabrications, and he was willing to cross them out; that bond that erects a wall between a married couple and the rest of the world had manifested itself. As they stood here in the lofty hall, it was no longer a concerned father and a conscientious nurse against a flighty wife. It was husband and wife against the clumsy intruder. She had lost.

So now what? She could make a dash for the stairs, even though by what seemed imperceptible movements the two of them now seemed to be standing directly at its base. She could push them aside and hurtle two steps at a time up the wide staircase, and up at that landing where the stairs divided, intuition might or might not direct her to the appropriate side, and after that to the particular closed door out of the undoubted many closed doors which would be the one she wanted. But she had a sense of listeners, watchers. Before she got to that spacious landing with its tufted window seat, someone would intervene. As they stood here in uneasy abeyance, in fact, the butler for no perceivable reason emerged from behind a door. Perhaps not a butler at all, but one of those detectives prepared for just such a troublemaker as Miss Brandt.

Besides, maybe she was wrong about the whole thing. Maybe the wild story she had concocted was just that. Wild. Disordered fantasy. The product, as Wilkerson would have been the first to point out, of loss, of emptiness, of desperation. Maybe Rosalie had in truth been alarmed by a kidnapping threat, and that was the reason, the only reason, she was insisting on this trip that mandated yet another ordeal for a man who had just returned from a brutal one.

Because what did she, Linda, have to go on? Bits and pieces of suspect clues, plus the muttered calumny of a disgruntled nurse, plus the discrepancy of a single day in a couple of loosely calculated dates. She had seized on the idea that Maxine was party to a nasty scheme, and look how wrong she'd been. Now, in the machinations of this serenely beautiful house, she discerned a plot even nastier, more bizarre, and she might be equally wrong.

All right, give up. Give up, and they will take their matched luggage and their collapsible baby seat and their unseen baby to whatever haven Rosalie has decreed as seemly, and that will be the end of it.

She moved to the front door, her hand was on the door knob just as the doorbell rang—when she opened it, Lenny burst in. Lenny with his face set in sternness, his gaze oblivious of anyone in the hall except her.

"Hey, listen. What's taking so long!" His voice rang out with rasping urgency.

"Lenny?"

"They just called from the office. Mrs. Hanover has been calling them."

"Mrs. Hanover?"

"You know, in Plummers Bay. She said the rash on the baby's neck is different from what the doctor led her to expect, and she wants someone to look at it. And she's hysterical and the office says to get the hell over there right away."

Lenny stepped ceremoniously out of the way in order to let her walk out, but Dr. Stanhope got there first. He gripped her arm and then dropped it. "Look here. You go up to our baby first. She's right upstairs, I want you to see exactly—no, Rosalie, I insist. That hysterical Mrs. Someone will have to wait. If my baby has a condition, I want to know what's what."

He moved with inspired speed. Five months in that fierce climate, but it had vitalized him—he crossed the large hall in half a dozen strides and pushed Rosalie's hand off the banister before she could gather herself for a fresh onslaught; when Linda followed, she was conscious of Rosalie being at least three steps behind. At the landing, where the window seat stretched under the casement window, he hesitated as if he had momentarily forgotten the floor plan, but maybe the pause was just to make sure Linda was behind him. Then he turned left, his footsteps again thudded on the carpet, and when he reached the top, it was left again. The door was closed, just as she expected, but without regard for a sleeping baby, he flung it open.

Except the baby was not sleeping. She was sitting in the crib, giving the small whimper that was not quite a cry but, to one who knew her, preliminary to one.

Linda knew her. The rosy mouth, the flat nose, the thin dark hair, the eyes deep with some indecipherable secret—the whole distinctive, delicious face. This time she was the one to do the pushing. Claude Stanhope had gotten to the crib before her, and she had to nudge him away with her shoulder so she could get in position to bend over the crib and grab the child under her arms and pick her up.

"Oh, my baby!" she cried. "Oh my God, Elena, Laney darling, I found you."

NINETEEN

"I STILL DON'T understand how you got on to it," Lenny said.

It was half past eight. The baby had been fed out of the red plastic dish and dressed in the fuzzy pajamas and put into the crib that a dilatory church group had neglected to pick up, and though the unwonted excitement and change of locale had occasioned some fretfulness, she was now sleeping quietly.

Linda sat down. She was exhausted. The exhaustion that leaves you keyed-up, quivering, energized, so you think you never will sleep again. "You know what? It was my fault for not getting on to it before. If I hadn't clung to that stubborn idea."

"Hey, Linda."

"True. A black market in babies—it was my holy thing. My great solution. The doctrine that made everything spin. I might still be holding on to it, but I found that Jay Earling had tried to kill me. He was the one, with his talent for mimicking a woman's voice— Irma Lynch let it drop. Why did he want me killed? Because after I went to his office pretending to ask his help in another adoption, he figured correctly that I was working on it, I wasn't going to sit passively back. Funny. I thought I was being the great deceiver, I could trap him. Me trap Jay Earling! He saw right through me. He recognized me as a menace, and if a real estate agent hadn't come—Lenny, I'll tell you about that later.

"Anyhow, after my second visit to Irma Lynch, I knew two things: about Jay as a would-be murderer, and also about Jay as Rosalie's lover. Her lover both before and after marriage. So there I was back to Rosalie again. The adorable, controversial Rosalie. The Rosalie who wouldn't let three women say good-bye to a baby, and also the Rosalie who wouldn't let a photographer take her picture. Only maybe it was not only her picture. Mrs. Stanhope and her baby, that poor dumb mistreated fellow had said. Well, why not? Why could a baby not be on view? Why did the possibility rouse her to such a frenzy?

"Okay. Then I thought about that kidnapping threat. That supposed kidnapping threat that she asked Wilkerson's advice about on October twenty-second. Should she get rid of her staff? But by the twenty-second, which was a Tuesday, the people had already been fired. First on Sunday night she did the deed, then she batted her pretty eyelashes at him and asked whether she should do it. Same thing with the Norris Employment Agency. I checked with Mrs. Norris. She called on Monday, by which time, of course, the women were already gone, but she didn't want the new staff till Tuesday afternoon. Why the delay? Who would empty her ashtrays? Who would cook her veal scallopini? For that matter, who'd take care of the baby? What was she waiting for? Just a second."

But when she went inside, all quiet in the crib. She pulled the blanket up another inch over the immobile shoulders, then she came back.

"So once I brooded about those discrepancies, I thought of what else had been happening on those days. With me, for instance. Me and Marylou. Marylou spreading the word on Monday that she'd have enough money on Tuesday to buy a car. And me falling into place like Jay Earling knew I would, a teenagers' counselor who could on no account get into a custody battle with a teenager—me giving back the baby on Tuesday. Tuesday noon. Which meant that their plan was now on track, the substitute baby was available, and Rosalie could set her scenario at the police station in motion.

"And when I started seeing it all as maybe connected—I mean, Rosalie's busy doing things with my baby—I thought of something else. That murder. Only not just any murder. A murder that involved water. Being submerged in water for a certain period. We'd taken for granted it was accidental, the baby just happening to be thrown into that pond along with Marylou."

"There are no accidents," Lenny said sententiously. "I forget what course I learned that in."

She looked at him. He might be a hero, but he was also a college freshman.

"Right. So I put that in too. Maybe far from being an accident, it was deliberate. The main point. A baby who, according to an autopsy, must have shown signs of having died from drowning."

She sat and then, restless, stood again. "So then I thought of Rosalie some more. First the Rosalie I'd seen at a dinner and then the one three women had presented. They had their differences, those women—two of them thought she was just as sweet and appealing as all get-out, such a helpless little dear—but they all agreed on one thing. She was a souse. She liked her cup of wine. Which of course squared with that blurry voice everyone had been so indulgent of at the dinner. Listen. Do you hear anything?"

"Not a peep. Linda, go *on*."

"So this helpless mother who's never without her little drinkie takes care of her baby on Sunday. Nurse's day off. What do you do with a baby, even if you're not especially thrilled by its company and not a pro at the whole business? You rock it to sleep. You give it a bottle. You feed it pablum or applesauce or whatever. And you"—she choked—"you bathe it. That's the nurse's routine, so when you're in charge, you follow it. And mostly it goes all right. But one day, when you maybe have an extra glass of wine before the bath..."

"Christ. You're not saying—"

She looked at him coldly, as if he was one of those who found Rosalie sweet and appealing. "Suppose she had. Drowned her baby, I mean. It happens. Not often, but once in a while a careless or inept or drunk

mother does it. Let's go for too long of that squirming little body. So what would Rosalie do, I wondered, if confronted with a baby who'd been allowed
to slip under. Would she call the police? A doctor? An
ambulance? Not on your life. She'd call her lover. Call
that smart, sleazy Jay Earling who understands everything right away. He knows that Claude Stanhope
is her valued meal ticket. His meal ticket too, if you
want to be precise—I saw the kind of practice he had;
in fact, I just found out that even the little he did for
the Center was got through Rosalie's intercession. So
maybe those two were planning to keep the current
arrangement, which in view of Stanhope's long ab-
sences must have had some plusses for them. Or
maybe, which I think more likely, Rosalie was biding
her time until on some grounds or other she could
wrangle the kind of divorce that would award her a
generous settlement. But either way, she wanted
Claude Stanhope's money. She needed his money. She
was desperate for his money to see her through the rest
of her life. And that money would on no account be
available to her if Stanhope knew what had happened
to his beloved child.'' Linda felt the urge, and resisted
it, to go once more into the room.

"So Jay and Rosalie work out a few basic facts.
Stanhope will be home on Friday night. However, because he left home when his child was six days old, at
which age most babies look like indeterminate blobs,
any girl child of roughly the same coloring and ap-
proximately the correct age will satisfy him. Jay Ear-

ling just happens to know a child of the desired characteristics. This child might, with some snappy maneuvering, some fancy exploits, be procured. And, a final imperative, everyone who would detect the difference between the original child and the surrogate must, on one pretext or other, be got out of the way."

For a second, Lenny didn't speak. His transparent face wore a dumbfounded protest; nothing in those freshmen courses had prepared him for this. "But Linda, you talked about an autopsy. Wouldn't an autopsy—"

"Tell the difference? To whom? To the police? The medical examiner? They don't know what the dead baby is supposed to look like. Besides, footprints are the only sure identification for a baby that age—footprints that are taken at birth—as Earling must have known, after a good period in stagnant water, which that pond is, footprints would be obliterated. If, that is, they even bothered to check."

"But when you saw it, didn't you—"

"I didn't see it. I saw the clothes—my baby's clothes. The clothes of the child Earling had carried off from my house. Another of my idiot mistakes. They asked did I want to look, and dumb me, indulging myself, going soft, I said no."

"That Earling, how did he manage everything?"

"Easy. Easy for someone of his slimy persuasive talents, I mean. 'That's not my only trick,' he said to Rosalie—he wasn't kidding. First he gets hold of that

poor nervy gullible Marylou and he promises her the
earth if she'll go through with the designated cha-
rade. Then when we all fall neatly in line, he hands my
baby over to Rosalie, and he takes that dead baby he's
been keeping since Sunday night"—Keeping where?
A refrigerator? A deep freeze? Don't think about it—
"and he dresses it up in Elena's white coverall with red
dots and red jacket with pink and green flowers and
white bonnet. And then to wind it all up, he meets
Marylou and kills her and dumps the two of them in
that pond." Her throat was dry; outrage carried her
along. "Which is something else that should have
given us pause. Because the pond is wholly inconve-
nient for someone driving up in a car. Hiding them
under a bush would have made more sense. The police noticed it, but they also muffed it. Or anyhow they
didn't follow through on it."

"And then he kills that girl. Jenna," Lenny said.
"A crazy mixed-up kid who never did a thing to him.
How'd he know she'd been with Marylou anyhow?"

"Her roommate told the police she had a scheme of
blackmail. Blackmail of who? Who else but Jay Earling? It would have been like her. She was reckless
without being smart, and headstrong without knowing caution. I can just hear her. 'Hey, Mr. Earling.
Marylou's got all this money, and she told me some
things about you, so how about you fork over a couple of thousand for me too.'"

"I don't care what she did. Blackmail, anything—
he shouldn't have shot her. Christ, what a rat."

She could understand. Jenna was real to him. Perhaps the only real item in this parade of second-hand items. He had driven her home, listened to her delusive hopes, fitted her into one of the categories defined by his Psychology 103-104 class. She was a person, not something pieced together from spare glimpses and questionable logistics. Stung into fervor, he walked up and down railing at Jay Earling.

"Look. He masterminded this, it's true; Jay Earling, tricky murderer. But that Rosalie, they better ring her in on it too." Rosalie who a few hours ago had laid her hands in pretty solicitation around her husband's shoulders, had stood, an adorable obstacle, at the foot of the stairs, had come within a hair's breadth of succeeding in her plan to get the baby permanently out of range.

"Don't think she was any helpless little waif. Look at the way she fired those people. Cool as anything, telling them no, they couldn't see the baby to say goodbye, when all the time there was no baby there. And then the act she put on at the Center dinner, when she compared her own darling baby at home, which of course was my baby, with Marylou's drowned child, which, God help us, was hers. And then"—the fury didn't let up—"then putting over on Wilkerson that slick story about finding a kidnapping message in a kitchen wastebasket. A wastebasket, for God's sake. There she sits, that defenseless kitten, and that cynical police officer actually falls for it."

"I still don't understand about that kidnapping," Lenny said. "Why did she have to go to all that trouble?"

"Window dressing. Necessary window dressing. To satisfy the police, of course, if trouble arose about the firings, but most of all to con her husband. The way he felt about that child, you think he'd have left her lying all day in her carriage on the south lawn? A place where no one could see her? Not him. He'd have picked her up and carried her off to a friend's house. Or maybe downtown to show her off. Or even to one of his meetings. Or if some newspaper photographer came around, he'd have said, Take my baby's picture too. I mean, those were the dangers Rosalie must have turned over in her busy head. And she couldn't risk it, any more than she could risk it with that young photographer. Couldn't take the chance that someone who knew what either her own child or mine really looked like might have been in position to get some funny ideas. So she makes up this slippery confection—it's really not bad, when you think about it—and she puts her cheek next to him and tells him, 'I know you've been away for six months, Claude darling, and all you want is to settle in at our beautiful home, but think of the danger to our baby from those unknown kidnappers, you never know how people like that will strike, we're only safe if we leave the country for a good long while.'"

Linda stopped. Imagine that. She can sound as vicious, as hating, as that nurse Irma.

"Poor Dr. Stanhope," Lenny said.

She shook her head, but the scene stayed with her. The scene that did not bear thinking about. A scene that had started, indeed, with Stanhope being the worst of the problem. "Put her down," his voice had thundered at Linda as she bent over the crib. "Are you out of your mind! Woman, put that baby down!" It was Rosalie, rushing in, seeing her worst nightmare take shape, who gave the game away. She didn't immediately come through with the truth. But she broke down. She babbled. She raved. "Oh, Claude, you mustn't think...really did try...happened so fast...not my fault at all..." It took a while, between Rosalie's ravings and her, Linda's, interjections, but when he got it, when the full sense of what had happened assaulted his mind, he simply walked out. He took his hunched-over shoulders and his broken face and left the room.

He recovered after that. To the unobservant eye, at least, he recovered. He was the one who called the police, asked the incriminating questions, set the course of retributive justice on its heavy-handed course. But what she would never forget was the last glimpse she had of him. Sometimes television captures the face of mortal suffering. "Tell me, Mrs. Smith, how do you feel about having seen your husband and three children burned to death," and on the screen, for a second, is flashed a face without restraints. You shouldn't see that face, you think. You have no right to. You're intruding on sacred territory.

That was how she felt when she finally left. She was carrying the baby, and she dropped an involuntary kiss on the loved head as she ducked into the car, and turning back for a second, she saw Claude Stanhope watching from the door. Linda the intruder, barging in on someone else's naked misery.

Lenny, whose own view had been from the nonparticipatory sidelines, hadn't quite finished lining up the facts. "That stuff about a reaction to the immunization, what was it?" he wanted to know.

It reminded her that another inspection was in order—this time she didn't resist the urge. She lifted the blanket, studied the position of the bent legs, ran a finger over the exposed cheek. Then she came back. "A slight reaction. It can happen. But all it does, in a few cases it causes a little swelling or maybe a slight rash. It's nothing you check with a flashlight to see how the pupils dilate, and it doesn't, perish the thought, impair the muscular system, and there's no kind of check after ten days, and also no serum to combat the noncondition. But once I found out she never went to the pediatrician herself, I was on my own. Freewheeling. I could make it up as I went along. And as for Dr. Grolier—"

"Dr. Leon Grolier of Boston," Lenny said. "No such person? Hey, pretty neat."

"Listen. You were no slouch yourself." Because, according to what he had told her, he had listened at the open window beside the front door, and when it struck him that she was going to be bested, he made his move. Since choice, as his pedantic voice explained, consists in tipping the balance of power between two cues, he simply reinforced the instigative power of the cue for Dr. Stanhope's affirmative action by ringing in other people with the same stimuli—something else he learned from Psych 103. It just showed how your schoolwork could have benefits you never dreamed of.

"Lenny, one of these days don't you have to go back to school?"

He was going tomorrow, he said. He'd just heard from his father. Grandpa off the critical list. Which meant Harold would be back tomorrow night.

But as he moved toward the door, another thought. "Hey, Linda. All that garbage I said at the beginning..."

She waited.

"About, you know, stepmothers. Against them. You'll forget that, won't you?"

What she had forgotten was Harold. Harold who had asked her to marry him, an eventuality which, as she'd said to Fran, was out of the question. But in the three days since he'd been gone, a new Harold had been proffered. One who didn't conform so simply to the image of amiable dentist making practiced small talk with his affluent clients. One, in fact, who hugged to his heart some bruising frustrations and unsuspected drives. "My dad's idea of heaven—him alone in the lab with one hundred test tubes of saliva," Lenny had said. It put Harold in a whole new light. It gave him the kind of sensibilities a woman might well be tempted to take on.

But suppose that taking was no longer available to her. Suppose circumstances had foreclosed that particular option. As she could not explain to Lenny, Harold's offer of marriage had been made when it seemed she no longer had a child. But now she has one. Oh, yes, she very definitely has one. In view of this stupendous alteration, would Harold care to renew his plea? After their strenuous collective efforts, Lenny might consider it a great thing to be her stepson, but when he saw how the wind had changed, it was anyone's guess whether Harold would still wish to be her husband.

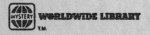

ERIC WRIGHT

"Clap hands, here comes Charlie... in Eric Wright's excellent series."
—*New York Times Book Review*

IT'LL MAKE A KILLING AT THE BOX OFFICE...

Acts of sabotage are throwing a major film off financial kilter. Inspector Charlie Salter finds his glamorous job as watchdog turning sinister as fake fire alarms, muggings, damaged equipment, stolen film and the kidnapping of an actor heat up production.

When the film's writer is found stabbed to death in a compromising position, Salter delves into underlying layers of greed, ambition and burning revenge as he races to find a killer who will stop at nothing to kill the film... or anybody who gets in the way.

"Charlie Salter is a likeable and savvy police veteran."
—*Publishers Weekly*

NOT AVAILABLE IN CANADA

FINAL

MYSTERY WORLDWIDE LIBRARY

FINAL CUT

THE UNDERGROUND STREAM

VELDA JOHNSTON

AN OLD HOUSE... WITH EVEN OLDER SECRETS

For twenty-four years, Gail Loring has fought both her fear of the alcoholic haze in which the women of her family have lived *and* the haunting images of a man—her great-great-great-grandfather—called the Monster of Monroe Street.

Now Gail can run no longer. At her ancestral home in the summer resort town of Hampton Harbor, she vows to confront the past. She finds herself stepping back into the stream of time. She is Martha Fitzwilliam, a young wife and mother who lived here more than a hundred and fifty years ago. Gail shares Martha's secrets... and feels her terror. A terror she must pursue to its ultimate act of shattering violence....

"The vicissitudes of time and place are skillfully evoked in this eerie and often dream-like novel."

—*Publishers Weekly*

 WORLDWIDE LIBRARY®

STREAM

COFFIN UNDERGROUND

First Time in Paperback

Gwendoline Butler

FOR THE TWISTED AND TALENTED, MURDER IS A GAME

Scotland Yard Chief Superintendent John Coffin is properly skeptical of the evil reputation of the house at No. 22, Church Row. True, the house has seen violent death over the centuries. None of it suspicious. Until now. Malcolm Kincaid, student. Bill Egan, recidivist. Terry Place, villain. Edward, Irene and Nona Pitt, victims. Phyllis Henley, policewoman. Why have they died?

Coffin suspects something more than a haunted house. He sees a human, complex web of relationships, interlocking and interacting in a way he can't yet fathom, one in which people get caught up and destroyed—as they play into the game of a very clever killer.

"...appealing hero...a gripping tale of sinister fantasy role-playing and bloody murder, sure to be relished."
—***Booklist***

NOT AVAILABLE IN CANADA

MYSTERY WORLDWIDE LIBRARY®

COFUND

A
Li*V*ely

A CHIEF

INSPECTOR

Form
MORRISSEY

of
MYSTERY

Death
KAY MITCHELL

First
Time in
Paperback

VICIOUS RUMORS

Marion Walsh, the town's local femme fatale, loses her housekeeper to a bottle of poisoned milk—a bottle most likely intended for her. Helen Goddard, whose husband, Robert, had been shamelessly seduced by Marion's charms, is the logical suspect, especially after Marion *is* brutally murdered.

But Chief Inspector Morrissey begins to sense something twisted and evil, something beyond the obvious love triangle everyone seems willing to accept—particularly after a convenient suicide and confessional note.

"... well-plotted, tersely scripted first novel."

—*Publishers Weekly*

NOT AVAILABLE IN CANADA   FORM

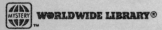 **W⊕RLDWIDE LIBRARY**® ™